Sir Knight of the Splendid Way

by

W E Cule

* * *

Illustrated by J Finnemore, R.I.

First published by (Lutterworth Press), 1926

Contents

The star was a face that looked on him tenderly.

I. THE ADVENTURE OF THE CHAPEL IN THE VALLEY

I

On the farther frontier of the Western Lands dwelt Sir Fortis, an aged knight who was warden of one of the outposts of the Great King. He had won high renown in the battles of his earlier days, but the virtues of his riper years had brought him glory of a gentler kind. The King's banner flew proudly from his castle wall, and when he rode forth he did honour to the royal service by the dignity of his bearing and the brightness of his arms: yet he did that service more honour by the kindness of his heart and the grace of his deeds. His castle was no less a place of pity than a place of power, and his judgment-seat was radiant with the light of mercy.

This good knight was well loved by his household, and by the young men whom he had trained in arms and chivalry. Of these the first was Constant, who had been page to Sir Fortis and was now his squire. He held the old knight in reverent worship, and because he reverenced his master he reverenced also his master's overlord. Ever and anon came royal messengers to the warden's castle, and ever and anon he saw men ride bravely by on their way to the City Beyond the Hills. The Service wooed him strongly, so that he dreamed night and day of great deeds for a great sovereign. Thus it came about at last that no knight set out on the King's Way but the heart of Constant followed him. Sir Fortis saw this, for he loved the boy well. "I know what is in thy heart," he said one day. "Is it not the King's Service and the Great City?"

"It is in my heart and my dreams," said Constant. "Yet I know myself ill-fitted for an enterprise so high. I have seen the worth of the King's knights, and it is far beyond my power."

But Sir Fortis smiled. "Which of us all is worthy?" he said. "Yet who is there that may not be made worthy? I have watched thy longings for many days, and I bid thee fear nothing. It will be my joy to set thee on thy way."

Then Constant's cheek's flamed and his eyes glowed. The old knight smiled as he saw it. "To me may it be given," he said in his heart, "to come at the end of the day to the King's presence, bearing my young men. May the King grant it!" And he said aloud:

"Soon my charge here must be delivered up, and myself summoned to see my lord face to face; but now it is my glory to lead thee to that Service which every man who enters must enter for himself. To that mystic place shalt thou go which is called the Chapel of Voices, and there shalt thou watch by thy arms, bearing with a high courage all that the night may bring. And there, if thou be true and steadfast, thou shalt see that vision without which no man can be worthy of the Great Name."

II

Sunward of the Western Lands lies the vale which is called the Vale of Promise. It is fair and fertile, with many sunny meadows and singing streams, and with flowery paths that seem to offer an easy journey through those Eastern hills which catch the first beams of the morning sun. So lovely are the peaks of those heights on sunny days soon after dawn that the eager heart of youth has often mistaken them for the turrets and pinnacles of the City Splendid, the City the Great King. But the aged and prudent have smiled at this, for they know that the City lies far beyond.

Many of the paths in the vale are merged at last in one, and this leads to another valley, still going Eastward. Here Constant found the way stern and stony, and there were no sunny meadows to tempt the traveller; yet a small stream still murmured by the way, and ever and anon a bed of flowers smiled among the rocks. And though the valley narrowed more and more, yet at times the path climbed high the cliff side, and gave a glimpse of lordly peaks shining gloriously.

At sunset the Chapel stood before him, set in the very heart of the pass. The one worn path came to its threshold, so that there was no onward way save through the Chapel. Still and strange and solemn it stood, but as he stepped over the threshold his tread called ghostly whispers from the stony walls. Lonely the Chapel seemed, but it was not silent.

Within all was plain and stern, but not without nobility. It had one casement only, and this was in the Eastward wall, a lofty casement shaped in the likeness of a great cross. Before the casement stood a table of stone, and before the table a place whereon the watcher might kneel. Before the table also lay a suit of knightly armour, breastplate and gorget and greaves, helm and shield. And the shield lay face upward, showing the Emblem of the Great King, a white cross set in a sombre ground.

Now as the echoes of his footstep died away, Constant paused to listen; and it seemed as though a whisper circled from wall to wall. Then a voice came, clear and low:

"What seeks he here?"

And immediately another voice answered:

"He seeks the Splendid Way and the King's City." Then the first voice spoke again:

"Is he strong and of a good courage?"

"In the King's name he can do all," answered the other voice; and at that word Constant took heart, and went within the chamber. And the clear low voice spoke again:

"This is thy place. These are the arms of the King's service, and here shalt thou keep vigil till the morning."

As he heard this command he saw anew the strange loneliness of the Chapel, grey and solemn in the gathering shadows. There came also a chill breeze from the casement, and he heard those eerie sounds once more, the whisperings that came and fled so causelessly. Yet he stood, and took in hand the sword, leaning upon its hilt; for he must not draw the blade or don the knightly arms until the night had passed. And so he held him ready for his vigil.

Then night fell upon the valley, and a great silence reigned everywhere save within the Chapel: for as the darkness deepened the mystic voices gathered strength, as though they loved the night and silence. "What seeks he here?" said one, again and again; and again and again the answer came in low reverberations from the solemn walls: "He seeks the Splendid Way, the Splendid Way." Then the watcher's heart beat fast, and he gripped the hilt of the sword: for it seemed to him that the answer was followed by a sound of a mocking laugh. And so the night began to pass, not in peace and rest but with the ceaseless traffic of unseen tongues. They came as the night wind when it whispers among the leaves; but the wind speaks and passes on, and no man fears the message that it bears; but the voices of the Chapel came with awe and warning, to riot in the chambers of thought and to try the soul in its inmost citadel.

Still Constant bore him bravely, for he had not come thus far to be turned by whispers. Yet as the voices grew more urgent his heart began to be moved and his hands were chilled upon the hilt they clasped. And so slowly the first hour fled.

Now there were two voices that spoke often, one with question and one with answer. "'What seeks he here?" asked one; and the other answered softly: "The Splendid Way and the City of the Great King." But as the night grew cold he heard less of the second voice, for it grew faint and uncertain: and at last there followed it a whisper that was like the stir of a foul wing in the darkness:

"The City of the Great King? How shall he ever find it?" Then the mocking laughter passed once more, and again the whisper followed it: "How shall he ever find it? And who comes back to tell that he has found it? Let him look and see the Splendid Way."

Then Constant, chilled to the heart, lifted his eyes and looked out through the casement. There was now an utter darkness, with no glory of moon or stars; yet as he searched the gloom, there came a faint, pale light, showing him the whole course of the Splendid Way. It was a narrow and winding way, and it wandered into deep valleys, shadowed and sorrowful, where the steel of foemen glimmered by the wayside; it rose to wild and barren mountain slopes where man must walk alone, for solitude brooded over them. Here it was lost to sight in the depths of a mighty forest, and there it hung like a slender thread over an awesome precipice. And when he discovered the end of the way his heart sank indeed, for there was no gleam of glory from a City Splendid The path was lost in the mists of a dark and dolorous valley, and he could not see that it ever came out again. For the other side of that last valley was beyond his vision.

"See the Splendid Way," said that deadly voice. "And now return and save thyself. The door stands open still."

But that counsel was too craven for the soul of knighthood. Constant gripped the hilt and pressed it to his bosom: and that silent cry was not in vain, for it brought back the friendly Voice that had answered for him at the first. "Be strong and fear nothing," it counselled him. "In the King's Name thou canst do all." And the echoes of the place answered softly, "All, all, all!"

Like a trumpet peal was that word to the young man's heart. He turned again to face the casement, with his back to the open door. The walls of the chamber had begun to tremble, as though they would part asunder, but they stood firm once more. The strange light faded from the way, and its terrors were sealed in darkness. Even the evil whispers for a time were stilled, so that it seemed that a great peace had fallen upon the whole valley.

8

But the peril came anew, in a form even subtle and deadly, "Constant," cried an ardent voice, "where art thou, Constant?" And in at the open door came the gallant Eagerheart and the loving Joyance, two squires of Sir Fortis and his own comrades from boyhood. Clear and fresh rang their voices through the gloom of the lonely Chapel.

"Was it not well that we followed so far?" cried Joyance. "Is it hither that thy dreams have led thee? But it is not yet too late, and we will take thee back. Too soon hast thou dared the way of the lonely heart."

"Even so," cried Eagerheart. "It is not that we would hinder thee when the true time comes. Nay, we will then go with thee, comrades still. Let the matter wait awhile till we be ready. Our good lord will be right glad for this."

Now Constant was sorely shaken, for thought of the days of love and play and dreams that they had passed together. Since his face was set to the Quest those joys must lie behind, and his journey must be lonely in the lack of them. The touch of Joyance was upon his shoulder, the warm breath of Eagerheart upon his cheek. Half he rose, and some swift word of friendship sprang to his lips. But in that perilous moment he saw at his feet the good shield whose emblem was the Emblem of the Great King, so the word that came was stern and strong.

"It is not Joyance and it is not Eagerheart," he cried. "They had never spoken so! Leave me in peace, in the Great Name!" And even as he spoke the tempters vanished, and he was alone. "In the King's Name," he said, "I go forward!" And once again came Peace, spreading her wings over valley and Chapel and giving quiet to his heart.

So he knelt down again beside the armour and saw the Emblem upon the shield, that it glowed as though some strange light had touched it: and then, looking up to see whence that light might come, he saw a heartening sight. At the head of the shadowy

9

casement shone a single star, faint and far away at first, but clear and friendly, like the voice of a comrade in the hour of peril. Then as he watched the star he was given the Vision of the Face.

It seemed that the small star became a great star, shining, radiant with promise, upon a sleeping world. In his spirit he left the Chapel of Voices and followed the star along a way that the Splendid Way. Long he followed, and at last the star seemed to wait for him, so that he might draw near. But when he drew near there was no star; for the star was a Face that looked upon him tenderly. Down-bent eyes were fixed upon his own, eyes whose love could not be measured, whose compassion was greater than life or death, whose love could compass land and sea, and time that was and is and shall be. About the brow was a dark crown, and the countenance was drawn and pale, but above all was that unutterable love and tenderness. When Constant saw it his heart leaped and burned, and his face shone with the glory that he saw in those matchless eyes. Fear was forgotten, and doubt, and the shadows of the Chapel were but a fleeting fancy: for all that he cared was to kneel and gaze, fearing to move lest the Vision should depart.

Nor did the Vision leave him, but stayed with that deep and tender power till all his heart and soul were won. Then lo! there was a great star at the head of the casement, the morning star, whose radiance gave a silver halo to the Vision and lined the dark crown with jewels of light. And so the light grew about him, until a brave voice spoke from the doorway:

"Rise, Sir Knight, for it is morning!"

III

It was the voice of Sir Fortis, and it was that good knight in very truth who stood in the door way. Behind him stood Joyance and Eagerheart with the horses, and with loving smiles for the friend they loved. And it was day indeed, for the last of the night had gone while his heart had glowed with the Vision of the Face. Moreover the cross which had been but a casement window was now a wide doorway leading to the valley beyond the Chapel: and through this doorway came the first beams of the morning sun, touching the stern grey walls till they shone white. They fell also upon the heaped armour, so that the Emblem upon the great shield had a new glory, and the noble helm glowed with fire.

The old knight raised Constant, and embraced him. "I might not come with thee to the Chapel," he said lovingly, "and no man might share thy vigil. But it is permitted to me to set thee on thy way. For I know that thou hast seen the Vision."

"Even now it was here," said Constant. "I knew not that it had fled."

"The Service," said Sir Fortis, "is not a Vision but a Way. But now we will eat together and then I will arm thee. For such is the joy that I have craved."

He called the squires, and they came eagerly, to lay upon the stone table a white cloth of linen, with cups of silver and a meal of bread and wine. The two knights sat, and ate together, and drank, the squires serving them: and the white glory of the casement cross fell upon the cloth of the table, and the cups of silver and the red wine of the Feast of the Splendid Way. But to Constant there was much more, for his heart was still fired by the Vision of the Face: and so great was its power that there seemed to be Another at the rude stone table, Lord of the Feast, Giver of the Bread and Wine.

When the Feast was over, Sir Fortis rose. "It is my joy to arm thee now," he said, "and to give thee, in the King's Name, the stroke of knighthood. Greater joy than this can fall to no man."

11

So as the squires brought the armour the good knight took the pieces, and set them in place, and girded them safe and well for his friend, as no man knew better how to do. Then he set upon his head the helmet of tested steel, and last of all took up the mighty shield. "Its Emblem is of mystic power," he said, "for as thy heart is, so shall its radiance be. May it be ever a shining light in dark and dreadful battle, a rallying-point for the King's men in troublous days, a beacon of hope for the weak and forlorn. Yet ever remember this," he added. "These arms shall be thy aid in hour of need, but ever the Vision of the Face shall be thy lodestar."

So Constant took the shield, and kissed it, and laid it upon his arm: and after that he knelt beside the stone table, and the old knight drew his sword and gave him the touch that was the seal of knighthood. "Rise, Sir Constant Knight of the Splendid Way," he said. "In the King's Name!" And he rose, and took his Sword and it was girded upon him: and Joyance and Eagerheart looked upon him with a noble envy. They had loved him well, but never as they loved him now.

"And now," said Sir Fortis, "thou art armed, a knight indeed. Here, too, is the door Eastward, and the beginning of the Splendid Way. Look and see!"

Then the young knight looked, and saw how the path at the foot of the casement led away into the valley and beyond. Even as he looked as he was granted a sudden vision of the whole of the Way, the Journey Perilous of the night of vigil; but now it was wholly changed, for the sun of morning shone upon it, lighting the darkest pass and silvering the heaviest cloud. Far away, walking slowly, was a traveller, his face set to the Eastward Hills and his shield upon his arm. Slowly indeed he went, as though the Way were rough and toilsome: but it seemed to Sir Constant that there was a light upon his path, a light that was not the light of the sun. It seemed to him that this light came from the footprints of One who walked with the traveller, as though to be his comrade. The form he could not see, but be knew that he was there.

This was a marvellous thing to him, and he watched with anxious wonder: but never did that unseen comrade leave the traveller alone. When the path led into a gorge dark and exceeding difficult they were so close that none might walk between: when they trod the way of the cliff it was the same, though the path seemed far too narrow for two; and on the wild mountain slope there was no solitude, for they went as brothers side by side. But when the dark and tangled forest was reached the order was changed, for there the guide walked before, leading the way, a light shining from his footprints and his presence as a morning mist.

Still the knight watched, and at last saw the distant traveller come to the misty valley at the end of the way: but there the presence came even nearer, taking him by the hand, so that they passed into that darkness together. For a moment they were lost to sight, but then the mists began to move, and lifted, and showed a sudden Vision of a great city wall and the golden glory of many gates. With that the vision passed, and only the beginning of the Way was there.

And that was enough. Sir Constant stepped out from the casement door, the door of the Emblem, and set his foot upon the Splendid Way. They bade him God Speed, and watched him go till be turned and waved his hand in farewell.

The old knight answered the signal joyously but when the pages looked they saw that his cheeks were wet with tears. Still he said nothing and presently turned, and got to his horse, and led them home, leaving the grey Chapel standing lonely in the heart of the valley. But the tears upon his face were not the tears of sorrow but the tears of fellowship: for he knew well the perils of the Way, the Valley of Toil, the Pass of Tears, the smooth temptation of the City Dangerous, and the cold mists of the Sunless Sea. Moreover, though he had won through to peace and honour, well did he know the peril of the Black Knight and his evil brood, the peril that takes many direful and alluring shapes, some of them so secret that a man may not write them down. So his tears fell because he might not help the one he loved.

Still the Chapel stands lonely in the Valley of Decision, with its altar of stone and its casement that is a cross: and still young hearts come to the Chapel in the glow of holy desire, to the night of vigil and to win the Vision of the Face. For not until they have seen this may they take to themselves the arms of knighthood and set out upon the Splendid Way.

II. THE ADVENTURE OF THE FALSE SIR JOYOUS

I

THE traveller who met Sir Constant on the morning of that day was plain of dress and humble of mien. He bore the marks of labour, and was clearly one who knew the traffic of toil and the company of lowly folk; yet he wore his simple garb with grace, and there was dignity in his bearing. When Sir Constant greeted him he answered courteously.

"I see the badge of the Great King's Service," said the knight. "That Service is mine also. Shall we then journey together?"

"Surely," said the Traveller. "Glad am I to walk with those who will walk with me."

They went on together, and kept that companionship for the whole of the day. The stranger told the knight that he was a Carpenter, and that he often came a day's journey on that road. Moreover, he knew the road well, for he had companied many travellers who had passed that way to the City of the Great King. Some of their names he knew, for he kept them in his heart; and when Sir Constant questioned him he spoke gently of them, giving due honour to their valiant deeds and noble worth. Nor had our knight met any man who could speak of the Great King as this man spoke, or whose words bore so much of the music of hope and faith and courage. Nay, so greatly was he stirred in heart that he saw not the lowliness of the stranger's garb nor the marks of toil upon his hands.

"Truly," he cried, "this is a day of joy for me. Promise now that we shall travel together as far as thy course may lie with mine."

Then the Carpenter, smiling, looked into his face. "It is for thee to say, Sir Knight," he answered. "I will not leave thee if thou leave not me."

Sir Constant laughed in his gladness, and lightly promised. He found so great joy in the company of the stranger that the hours passed speedily, but there was more than joy in his heart. This humble traveller was wise in the counsels of the King, and held a rich treasure of noble thoughts; and as the day sped, it seemed to our good knight that this journey was as another which two men had taken long ago. One who seemed a stranger had joined them unawares, and by his words had made their hearts burn within them. In the evening he had sat at meat with them, and suddenly they had known him for the beloved Master whom they had lost. "Such a power has this Carpenter," mused the knight. "It may be that we shall rest for the night together; for he will not leave me as that stranger left his friends."

It was not thus that the night was spent. At sunset they drew near the end of the day's journey, and it was then that the stranger said: "A little way and we reach the cottage of a woodman who is known to me. If his home is not too humble, Sir Knight, it will hold a welcome for thee."

Sir Constant smiled at the thought, but ere the smile had left his lips the words were almost forgotten. For beside the road he saw a lordly gate, and at the gate two squires, standing and waiting. Beyond the gate in a spacious park stood a palace of marble, shaded by lofty trees and surrounded by beds of costly flowers. And even as he looked and wondered, the squires came forward and addressed him courteously.

"Fair knight," said one, "my lord, Sir Joyous, sets us here to greet and welcome any knight of the King's Service. He would claim thee as his guest."

"Where many of the Service have found rest and pleasure," said the other. "See, our lord comes to welcome thee." The knight looked, and saw a man of noble down to the gate. "Is not this a place where we may rest?" he asked of his friend of the day. "Let us go in."

"The welcome is for thee only," answered the Carpenter. "Me they have not asked."

Now the knight saw that this was so, and for the moment he was confused. Swiftly he remembered that this man was but a Carpenter, despite his gracious speech and gentle courtesy. In that instant the squires led him within the gate to meet their master.

Sir Joyous was courteous and gracious, richly clad and of a generous hospitality. He begged that the knight would honour his house, where he should meet with none but friends: for it was his joy, he said, to serve and shelter the King's knights. But when Sir Constant looked back to the gate, and spoke haltingly of his companion, this lord was filled with surprise.

"Is that a friend of thine?" he said. "Perchance he joined thee on the journey? He is a good fellow, but a Carpenter, and visits a certain woodman whose cottage stands a short space along the road. It is there that he will spend the night, but that is surely no place for thee. We have a knightlier lodging here."

Now those words worked so powerfully that our knight forgot his promise of the morning, and was almost ashamed that he should have companied with one so humble. Nor had he seen the baseness of his thought, for Sir Joyous took his arm to lead him, and at the same time there came from the palace the sound of ravishing music. So he suffered himself to be led, though more reluctant than willing: and when he once glanced behind he saw the Carpenter, with down-bent head, moving sorrowfully away from the gates.

II

When Constant found himself awake it was long past midnight, and the great house of Sir Joyous was dark and silent. For a time he lay confused, for the sound of music and song was with him still; but presently he remembered the chamber in which he lay. Then came the memory of his evening with the household of Sir Joyous, of the laughter that had echoed in the halls and gardens, and of the light words that had passed so freely as the company had sat at supper. For there were many guests at the table of the lord of the marble palace, resting awhile from the perils of the road or the labour of a weary task.

But as memory came he knew that his sleep had been troubled by anxious dreams, and now the thoughts of those dreams thronged upon him, so that he was beset by urgent questions. Through all the feasting he had kept himself sober and vigilant as became a knight of the Splendid Way; but he had seen others of the same service strangely heedless, as though no journey lay beyond the gates, no battles to fight, no wrongs to meet and conquer. But the pleasant Sir Joyous seeing the questions in his eyes, had spoken a wise word: "But see, this is a house of ease and rest. And are we not bidden to rejoice always?" And that subtle word had checked his doubts until he had gone to his chamber to sleep.

Now those doubts returned more strongly. It came to his heart that there had been little grace in his leaving the Carpenter, and also that he had never felt so far from the hand and power of the Great King. At that he was awake indeed, and sought to call back to mind that wondrous joy, the Vision of the Face; but he sought in vain, for the Vision seemed far away. A face came indeed, but it looked at him more in sorrow than in love, and he knew at last that it was the face of that humble Carpenter as he had seen him at their time of parting, turning away from the gate in patient silence and with down-bent head. Sorrowful and reproachful was that look, but so great was its power that at last he rose from his bed.

18

"I know not what I fear," he said in his heart. "But I must resolve my fears ere I sleep again." Now he found that he was not utterly in the dark, for at his bedside burned a small silver lamp which bore the name Reflection. By the light of the lamp he dressed himself, save for his armour, and took the lamp, and left the chamber. He remembered that in the great hail below he had seen a book upon a stand, a book that seemed to be a Book of the Counsel of the Journey. "If they keep and reverence the Book," he said, "they must be good and faithful servants of the Great King, and I shall fear nothing. But I must see before I sleep." So by the light of the lamp he made his way down the great staircase to the hall, and found the place and the book. The book bore the Emblem of the Great King upon its cover, and the same noble Emblem was emblazoned on a rich curtain which hung upon the wall behind.

Sir Constant went to the book, and opened it by the light of the silver lamp: but to his amaze he found that it was not what it seemed to be. In semblance a Book of the King's Counsel, it was a mockery within, for the words of the King's wisdom were changed and false. The counsels of toil and duty were not there, nor yet the counsels of love to the loveless and help to the helpless and succour for the needy.

He saw no sign of the King's joy in the soul that is meek and humble, or in the heart that gives itself for others or in the pity that cheers the lot of the burdened and afflicted. These the maker of the book had cast aside as though they grieved his spirit, and instead had chosen the tales of pleasant things, of the glories of the strong and of the might of kings. Of these things he had made a world that Constant knew not at all, a world that had no love but the love of ease and power.

Then Sir Constant, in mingled fear and anger, rent the book across, and cast the fragments upon the floor. Never again should its false counsels deceive any man! Then he took up the lamp and turned to the crimson curtain which hung upon the wall, bearing the royal Emblem.

"Perchance," he said, "they have here a picture of the Great King or of His City: but I fear me that it will be as false as the Book." And he drew the curtain aside, holding up the lamp so that he might see what lay beyond.

Now the picture hidden by the curtain was the portrait of Sir Joyous, the lord of the Palace, fairly painted and having his name beneath. Gracious and comely, he smiled from the canvas as he smiled upon his guests; and so friendly was the smile that for a moment Sir Constant was rebuked, remembering the courteous welcome of the man whose secrets he now sought to uncover. But even as this thought came, the light of silver lamp shone clearly on the portrait, and as the beams played upon the painted face the knight saw a strange and fearful thing. The face changed, the gracious courtesy faded away, greed and pride and gluttony shone from the eyes, and the mouth was foolish with the folly of wine. And at the shoulder of Sir Joyous stood a ghostly shadow that was at first a shadow only, dim and unformed; but as the knight moved the lamp to see better, the shadow took form, and became a man clad in mail, with sword and dagger drawn, and with evil eyes that shone fiercely through visor bars. And so strong was the menace in that glowering look and in the naked steel that Sir Constant started, and gave a cry, and drew back; so the curtain fell and the enchanted picture was concealed.

He needed not to see it again, for he knew that he had been warned of peril; so he ran back to his chamber, and with the silver lamp to aid him, donned his knightly arms. Then he left his room and went out to the corridor, eager to escape but resolved to know the plot of his secret foe. There was no man in the corridor, but afar off he saw a light from a door that stood ajar: so he took his shield upon his arm, and drew his sword, and strode down the corridor to the lighted doorway. On the rich carpet of that floor went silently, so that he had reached the threshold of the room before those within were aware of his coming.

They were two, and they sat at a table in the room with a chart spread before them. One was Sir Joyous, the lord of the Palace, not gracious and smiling now, but with craft and cunning in his eyes. The other was a knight who had sat at the board in the evening, far off from Sir Constant, but seen as a knight of great strength, and proud and haughty in bearing. He was not of the Royal Service, but a guest of Sir Joyous: some had called him the Black Knight, from the colour of his armour, and others the Knight of the Leopard, from the emblem upon his shield. But his true name was not spoken, for he was said to be under a vow to conceal it.

Now he wore a helmet, but had put off his heavy mail; and he spoke sternly to Sir Joyous, pointing to a place upon the chart.

"See, here in his path lies the Valley of Toil, where I care little to follow him. But if you keep him here even for a few days he will have little zest for such a place as that. Then, when he is wandering from the Way, I can come upon him at my leisure, and conquer him with ease."

"It is well planned," said Sir Joyous. "By fair words and promises I will seek to keep him here. That is my part. The rest I leave to thee. It is grievous to me to have those pestilent knights in my halls, but it is something for my pains that this is their road to doom."

Then they laughed together, an evil laugh laden with dark thoughts: but the laugh ended suddenly, for the Black Knight heard a sound at the door, and turned, and with a fierce cry drew down his visor; yet in that moment Constant had seen his eyes, and knew him for the evil knight of the picture in the hall. Then blustered the false Sir Joyous, like a friend who has been wronged:

"How is this, Sir Knight? Why that sword and this night walking? Is this the courtesy due to a house of friendship?"

Sir Constant eyed him scornfully, deigning no answer: for he saw that this palace was a place of treachery and deceit, and he longed with a great longing for the open air of the Splendid Way. "And woe is mine that I left that way," he said in his heart, "for now there may be great loss ere I win back to it."

So as the plotters sprang to their feet he turned to make his escape.

III

But an escape from the Palace of the false Sir Joyous was not so easy a thing. The alarm was already given, perchance by some watchman who had seen him go to the hall with his silver lamp, or by some who had found the torn book and had afterwards heard his armour ring as donned it: so he entered the great corridor again to find it alight with torches, and the sons of Sir Joyous and the servitors of the Black Knight coming to meet him. Some had pikes and halberds, some swords and battle-axes; and there was a great stir in the palace, so that the awakened guests began to come from their chambers. Then cried the false Sir Joyous behind—"Hold the way! Never let him pass!" and the Black Knight shouted that they should bring his armour. So Sir Constant, seeing his peril, braced his shield and lifted his good sword, and with a shout, "In the King's Name!" drove at the rabble mightily. So great was the shock of his attack that they were at first astonished, and gave back before him to the head of the stairs; and it was seen in that moment that the Emblem upon his shield glowed as with a heavenly fire.

Hard was the fight that he fought down the wide staircase to the cold hall, where the evil book lay still upon the floor and the emblazoned curtain still hung with the golden lie upon it. For every moment the press grew thicker as the men-at-arms came from their quarters, and had it not been for the advantage of the stairs it had been ill indeed for him. The clang of weighty blows, the crash of arms, echoed and rang about the marble pillars, and ruddy shone the red torches on the fierce faces and the motley dress of those who had had no time to don their mail. There our knight had the advantage, and, moreover, his fierce joy in the battle gave him added power; so he drove them before him strongly and parted them to right and left, giving them no time to recover or to make ready, and heeding not their cries and threats.

Least of all did he heed the voices of some who stood by, wearing the Emblem of the King's Service but putting out no hand to aid him. Nay, they called upon him to cease, for that Sir Joyous was a friend and not a foe; but his wrath rose at that base counsel, for he remembered the picture and the plot, and the enchanted book: and once more swinging his bright blade aloft, he struck with all his heart. So it was that he won his way to the staircase, and down to the hall; then to the door, where night loomed dark and still. There he fought so stoutly that the serving men dared not withstand him, and in a while he had the cool breath of night upon his brows and above him the heaven of stars.

But the struggle was yet to come. When the alarm had first been given they had brought the Black Knight his shield and sword and battle mail, so that he was fully armed. Now he came out, driving the press aside and bidding the sons of Sir Joyous make way for him. So they stood aloof, and the champion strode out upon the steps, wrathful and arrogant.

"The fight is mine," he cried. "Let me deal with him alone. And guard thee well, Sir Knight, for now there is only one way out."

So the servants and men-at-arms made a ring, ruddy with torches and grey with eager faces. Sir Constant braced his shield anew, and gripped his hilt with a firmer grip. There was much to do before the end, and that end he could not see. And the marble walls of the Palace looked down upon the fight, with Sir Joyous himself upon the balcony above the pillared door. He was no warrior, yet loved to see a battle to the death.

Then cried Sir Constant his battle cry, "In the King's Name!" and dashed forward, swinging high his sword. The Black Knight countered sternly, and then the dread fight swayed to and fro with the clang of steel on steel, and the ceaseless tread of mail-clad feet, and fierce, hard breathing through stifling helmet bars. And so fierce and equal was the struggle that Sir Joyous held his breath and the watchers fell silent in their watching.

Sir Constant gained some ground at first, so fierce was his attack; but the Black Knight was a master of arms, skilled in defence and patient to wait his time. When the first onset had spent itself he won back his lost ground steadily, his mighty shield and his threatening blade ever at the point of danger. And ever when Sir Constant slackened he pressed forward, the more ominous and terrible for his black armour and his cruel shield. So he became the attacker, forcing our good knight back and back, seeking with steady and relentless eye the opening for a deadly stroke. And Sir Constant, for all his dauntless courage, was oppressed by the knowledge that in the great throng of the Palace there was not one that wished him well.

Nor was the end long delayed, for presently he missed his stroke and for an instant left his head unguarded. Then the Black Knight struck hard, beating the sword out of his grip, so that it clanged loudly upon the paving of the courtyard: and though the fallen sword had saved a little, the weight of the blow was still so great that it brought the young knight to his knees, dazed and helpless. And the foe towered triumphantly above him, blade upraised once more.

"Now I have thee," he cried. "Yield thee to my pleasure."

But Sir Constant had no thought of craving mercy, though he knew that he was down.

"Not I," he cried bravely. "I will not yield even though I be slain.

"Oh, fool," said the Black Knight, "I seek a living slave, not a dead foe. Swear to serve me faithfully all thy days and I will surely spare thy life."

Sir Constant heard, but only faintly at first, so heavy had been his hurt: but kneeling there with his head bowed, spent and almost hopeless, he took the meaning of those foul words, and shuddered: for with them came the memory of Another whose Service he had taken and whose arms he bore. With that thought he raised his head to look up: and it seemed that a torch that danced before him ceased to move, and became a Star shining steadily and gloriously in a tall, narrow casement in a grey stone chapel. 'Then the Star was a Face, overflowing with pity, yearning in love, magnificent in courage; and as he saw it his tired heart leaped and swelled, and there came back to him in full flood the unspeakable Joy of the Vision of the Face. It passed into his veins like fire, and it was both fire and power. He put out his hand, and to his wonder it touched the hilt of his sword, fallen beside him. He seized it and sprang up, giving a great cry.

That cry was echoed in amaze by the watchers, the Black Knight stood back suddenly and lo! the fight was raging once more. But now our young knight had a power which none might withstand, the power of the Vision of the Face. It nerved heart and hand together, and his blows had the strong ring of triumph. Warily the Black Knight gave ground, waiting the chance that never came: for this time the onslaught did not slacken, but grew in fury, so that no blade could counter it, no shield withstand it, no helm be other than a vain defence. At last he was forced against the pillars of the door, beneath the balcony of Sir Joyous: and there Sir Constant, with another cry "In the Kings Name!" beat down his guard, and shore through his shield, and brought him crashing to earth. There he lay, groaning grievously, and a great cry rose—"He is down! He is down!"

The star was a face that looked on him tenderly.

Then came Sir Joyous, pleading for his life. "Spare him, good knight," he cried. "He is my kinsman, and I gave thee welcome."

"Who art thou that I should hear thee?" cried Sir Constant. "And who is he that I should spare him! Unlace his helm and let me see his face."

So they unlaced the helmet and removed it, for they dared not gainsay the conqueror. Sir Constant stepped forward, his sword ready, and looked into the face of the foe who had so sorely tried him. But when he had looked he gave a cry of amazement and horror and fear, for the face upon which he gazed was his own face, though now hideous with pain and rage and the heat of battle. It was his own face shown in a mirror of mockery and evil, but none the less his own!

Then said they that stood by: "It is his brother."

"Nay," said Sir Joyous, in a hush of wonder. "It is his own face."

But the Black Knight lay, a mocking smile upon his lips and defiance in his eyes. "I am down indeed," he said. "But canst thou slay me, Sir Constant? Strike, then, and make an end!"

But Sir Constant shuddered and shrank back, chilled to the heart and dumb: for he saw that here he had no foe to be easily destroyed, but a Sorcerer Knight of deadly power and guile. And as he stood confused, his heart heavy with the shadow of this unconquered peril, the henchmen of Sir Joyous pressed forward, and came between him and his foe, and raised the Black Knight, and bore him within the doorway. Then with many hands they thrust the doors together, and fastened them with clanging bars to the sound of mocking laughter.

IV

By the light of the stars Constant left the domain of Sir Joyous and found the road again, with great relief though in great pain. Yet a little while and he saw a light from the door of a cottage, the woodman's cottage of which the Carpenter had spoken. Moreover, the door was ajar, and the woodman was waiting at the door to greet him. He had heard the crash of battle afar off, and had known well what was afoot. And when Constant came thither he saw upon the open door the Emblem of the Great King.

"For this is one of His appointed rest-houses," said the man. "And my name is Joyous, Keeper of the house. Glad am I to serve Him by aiding thee."

He took the knight within, and relieved him of his armour, and laid balm upon his wounds. Then he brought bread and wine, and they sat together at the table while he unveiled the mystery of this grievous adventure.

"It was the King's will that thou shouldst rest here," he said, "for the rest-house of Joyous is one of the rewards of the Royal Service. But the Black Knight, the Sorcerer of many faces, subtle beyond all telling, has mocked this gracious provision and made of it a snare. He has placed that Palace by the way, and over it a fair-spoken warden to whom he hath given a name like mine. But the warden of the Palace is of the brood of the Black Knight, and when he has beguiled a traveller within, it is only that he may learn to his cost the evil power of his most deadly foe. So the Palace of the false Sir Joyous, often called the Palace of Pleasures, becomes the way to failure and dishonour.

"But even there the King hath power, and in every sleeping-chamber is a small silver lamp, the lamp which is called Reflection, which is the King's gift; and it is the holy property of this lamp that where its light is shed the false creations of the Palace must reveal their true form. Thus many good knights saved their life and honour, using the lamp and fighting their way out the Palace. So it was with thee, though sore and long thy battle."

Then said Sir Constant heavily: "That Black Knight is indeed a doughty champion. I fear that I have not yet done with him and his magic."

"Nay," said the Keeper of the King's rest-house. "Not yet, nor for many days. I called him a sorcerer and subtle, but no words of mine may tell his power and guile. One aim he hath, to win thee from the Royal Service; and though he be conquered many times, yet will be come again in other guise, pitiless and unrelenting, so great is his hatred for the Lord of the Splendid Way and His pure Service. Many will be his snares and his disguises, many are the helpers who serve him; but what danger can be greater than this, that he can bear the semblance of thy very self and speak with thy very voice in the inner chambers of thy heart? Nay, Sir Knight, there is but one way of meeting this unresting foe. It is by the Vision of the Face and by that alone. So shalt thou win through to do the King's Will, and honour His Service, and reach at last His City."

Then was Sir Constant sore in spirit for a time with the knowledge of a foe so greatly to be dreaded, and with shame of his own folly in being so ensnared; but Master Joyous gave him aid by calling up precious memories and noble thoughts, of which he had a treasure gathered through the years. At last, therefore, our knight went to his rest greatly heartened: and in his rest, because he had sought it, the Vision of the Face came to him again, shining through his dreams, tender and resplendent. It was more than balm for his soreness of heart, and in the morning he faced the new day with new power. Moreover, he knew that one great peril, the snare of this false Sir Joyous, could lure him no more.

So it was that when he set out he looked not at all to the palace of marble that lay in the park behind, but turned his face steadfastly to the road which led to the Valley of Toil and the Pass of Tears. For the Carpenter, said Master Joyous, had gone that way.

"Beat down his guard and shore through his shield."

III. THE ADVENTURE OF THE LOST SIR ARDENT

I

THIS city by the way was a place of much delight and comeliness. Its gates of silver stood wide against their marble pillars, and the walls and towers were decked with flowers and clothed with vines. Nor was there any sign of arms to check the peaceful traveller, for there were no guards at the gate, no sentinels upon the walls. Moreover, on the pillar of the gate stood a proclamation in letters of gold "For the pilgrim of the Splendid Way there is rest and peace in this city, the City of Good Intent."

Sir Constant came here on a day at noon, and the place seemed very gracious in the midst of the dusty way. Yet before he would enter he gave thought to the matter, for he could not remember that such a city had been named as one of his resting-places. But there was in this region a City called Dangerous, and he feared that this might be the same: so he sat down on a grassy bank without the gate, and took his refreshment there while he watched all that went on.

There was little stir about the gate, for it seemed that the city was a place of rest rather than a place of traffic. Ever and anon one would come up, and read the proclamation, and go in, but he could not see that any came out. Within were gardens and fountains, and pleasant roads shaded from the sun, but there was no thunder of hoofs, no sound of toil, no clang of martial arms. He saw men pass along the shaded roads or linger by the fountains among the flowers, but they moved quietly, with peace upon their brows.

But ere he had waited long he saw a strange thing. There was a lodge by the gate, and beside the lodge a great bell. In a little while an old, stern man came out of the lodge, and took the rope of the bell, and rang, so that suddenly a great clamour burst upon the air and rolled far along the sunny ramparts of the city. Clear and mighty, urgent and commanding, was that brazen voice, so that the

31

silver gates rang with the sound, the trees quivered, the walls and towers gave sonorous answer. In the city men paused and looked up, and listened some striking their hands upon their brows in sudden, bewildered awakening, while others quickened their steps as though to escape the sound. But soon the bell ceased its clamour, the echoes slowly died away, and there was a great peace upon that strange and silent city.

The old man, having rung his bell, would have entered his lodge again, but Sir Constant went up to him eagerly. For he had seen that the ringer wore the Emblem of the Great King.

"I am of the same Service," he said, "and I would not enter the city lest it should be the City Dangerous. Tell me, I pray thee, the story of the city and the bell."

Kindly the old man looked upon him, marking his gallant shield and his attire stained with the dust of the way. "It is well that you enter not this city," he said. "Those who enter it fall under its spell, which is a deadly spell. Full many a gallant knight hath ventured there, thinking no evil: but he comes out no more."

"Yet it is a fair city," said Sir Constant.

"In all thy journey thou shalt not find a fairer," said the old man. "Some say that it is as beautiful as the City we seek, far over the Eastern Hills. But its danger lies in its beauty and its fair welcome to the traveller: for who shall look for peril when he sees only peace and rest and welcome, with no sign of: arms or toil or chains? Yet the spell is a power that hath held captive the strongest heart; and this city is one of the most false and deadly of all the perils that beset the knights of the King's Service. For the victims of the spell dream of great and noble deeds, and know not that they are dreaming only: and while they dream the swift hours fly, and the crowding years, until their time is gone. And through the spell of this city they never find the City Beyond the Hills."

"And the bell?" said Sir Constant. "Is this by command of the King?

32

"It is, Sir Knight. By His command am I set here, and the bell, and ever and anon I ring the bell to rouse the dreamers. Nay, I go sometimes into the city and seek those who are lost, and entreat them to come forth. But they love me not, for they love their dreams: and it is with anger and scorn that they drive me forth, So here I stay, with my bell, and seek to wake them from their sleep. Some hear me, and wake, and take up their arms, and I send them on their way with great joy. But these are few indeed, so deadly is this enchantment."

"And is there any service that I may do here?" asked Sir Constant.

"If there were one in this city who loved thee well, thou mightest serve him," said the old man. "The voice of love is oft more heeded than my bell. Tell me, whence art thou and who were thy friends?"

Then Constant told him of Sir Fortis, and lo! the old man knew him. "A great and noble knight," he said, "whose name is renowned throughout the Way. Then shouldst thou know Ardent, who was also of the household of Sir Fortis."

"He was my friend and comrade," cried Sir Constant. "Has he passed this way?"

"Alas!" said the old man. "Many days past he came to this city, and read the proclamation on the gate, and dared to enter. Vainly I warned him, for he laughed my fears to scorn. But the days have passed, and the spell prevails, and Sir Ardent, fearless and gallant, is lost to the King's Service. Nay, I went into the city, and sought him and found him: but all my pleading was in vain, for such was the spell of his dreams that he could not understand my words."

Then was Sir Constant grieved to the heart, and hung his head for shame and sorrow. His faith in Ardent had been great, for the strong hope that was his, and the eager heart, and the gracious spirit: and it was to him a grievous thing that so fair a knight should have fallen thus.

"Tell me how I may serve Sir Ardent," he cried. "Shall I go and seek him? I would pass on and leave him here in peril."

"That is well spoken," said the old man.

"It is permitted to thee to enter the city, for there is a way to steel thy heart against its snare: and this can be if thou keep steadily before thee the Vision of the Face. And I will go with thee, and lead thee to the house of Ardent. But I bid thee be full of prudence and care, and of a humble heart, for the enchantment of this place is very deadly."

Then our good knight fortified himself with his love for Sir Ardent and his memory of the good Sir Fortis, whom he longed to please in this matter: but more than all he strengthened his heart with the memory of the Chapel of Voices, and the Face of Love that was the guide and the glory of the Splendid Way. Then he drew his sword and took his shield upon his arm and said, "I am ready." So the stern old man, walking closely at his side, led him in by the open gate.

II

Within the city there was no man who questioned them of their business or sought to stay their journey. There were many men, but each seemed to live in his own world, taking knowledge of no other. They smiled as they passed but it was a smile of the lips only, for their eyes were full of dreams. And everywhere was peace and the fragrance of flowers, and glowing sunlight and pleasant shade. There was no sound of hoof or axe or hammer, no stir of haste, no whisper of unrest. On that peace and stillness the tread of mailed feet broke with startling sound.

"But here is no danger of arms," said the knight, in a little while. "Therefore may I sheathe my sword."

"Nay," said the old man. "Keep the sword drawn. It hath another use than warfare. Some may see it and remember."

Then the air of the city enfolded them, and it was a shroud of warmth and sweetness and languor. The knight breathed it, and for a moment rejoiced in it: but in a little while he felt the weight of his arms, that they oppressed him greatly. Never had that stout shield seemed so weighty, the mail so cumbersome; and when he looked he saw that others had felt the same oppression, for no man in that city bore arms. Some of them had the bearing of knighthood but they had doffed their armour, and went about lightly in silk and linen. So presently be said to the old man:

"There is no danger here, and the air oppresses. I will leave my shield, therefore, and other pieces of my mail, and take them up when we come back this way."

"Nay," said the old man, "for then thou wouldst never come back this way. What but an evil spell would rob thee of thy arms?"

Then the knight remembered how he had won his arms, and how they had served him nobly and well, and a hot shame burned him. And when some of the dreamers saw him, tall in mail and helm, with the shield of the Emblem and the shining sword, they stood and gazed, filled with wonder and with troubled thoughts. And there were some who were roused from their dreams in this way, and later came out of the city and continued their journey.

Yet a little and our knight came to the Place of Glorious Vistas. He saw far before him, yet not so far, a path that led over the Eastern Hills, and at the end of that path a city more fair and glorious than any that man had ever seen. Its gates and walls, its pinnacles and towers, shone with a radiance like unto the light of the sun and it was so great in extent that the eye might not measure it. And ever up the shining path went the Knights of the Splendid Way, to be welcomed at the gates by guards in glowing white. Above the wall of the golden gate flew a banner, a banner of pure white, bearing an Emblem worked in gold, the Emblem of the Great King.

So glorious was this vision that Sir Constant was fain to pause. But the old man rebuked and forbad him. "They all see these things," he said. "All those who are lost to the Royal Service. Seek one vision only, for that is the vision for thee, and on to save thy friend!"

And even as he spoke the vision passed like a mirage, for at the words the knight had called back the Vision of the Face. There was nothing where the vision had been, save the trees and flowers of the city and its unceasing sunshine.

After this there were many enchantments both of thought and sight, but our knight denied them resolutely, keeping ever in his mind the Vision of the Face. They also met some who would have begged him to enter their houses for rest and pleasure, but here his guide was his guard; for when these citizens saw the stern old man they turned aside and went their way, making it plain that he was no welcome guest in that city. So they came without hurt through the sleeping streets to the house of Ardent.

It was a spacious house, and its gardens looked over the city wall to the plain beyond, bounded by cloudy hills. The door stood open, and there was none to stay them: so the old man led Sir Constant through the house to the gardens. On every hand was the beauty of the City of Good Intent in flowing tapestries and rich paintings, in flowers of many hues and many perfumes. Our knight saw paintings and the tapestries and wondered for the dreamer who dwelt here had adorned his house with all the glory of conquest. But there was nothing that spoke of dust of the way, or the heat of the sun at noon or the fainting heart that fears the morrow yet holds grimly to the rugged path. One only was the story that the pictures told.

They found Sir Ardent in an arbour in the garden, resting among a wealth of flowers He lay like a child after play, but they were sorry playthings that were strewed beside him—a shield discoloured by damp and dust, with little of its Emblem left to see; a sword half drawn, showing the blade rusted and ruined; a noble helm so marred that no man might wear it without shame. All his mail was

36

there, but it made so graceless a sight that Sir Constant's heart burned for it. As for Sir Ardent, he lay smiling and looking over the city wall to the hills beyond the plain: and in his dreaming eyes were visions that no other man might see. He saw Sir Constant, but with neither wonder nor welcome.

"Is it thou, old friend?" he said. "Gladly will I welcome thee when I have seen all. But wait a little while, for this glorious scene must not be lost. There is the Splendid Way, changed to a wide white road at last, and shaded by palms and orange groves. Far off, but yet not far, are the gates of the Great City, where a banner flies, the banner of the Great King. Can you not see?" But Sir Constant could not see, for there was nothing but a dreary plain beyond the wall. "Oh, Ardent!" he cried, "this dream of thine is an evil spell that must destroy thee. Awake and arise ere it be too late."

But Sir Ardent heeded not. "Hearken," he said. "Far off upon the Way walks a knight, a good knight and true, his shield upon his arm and his mail bright and shining. Never once hath he failed or faltered, and now the Great City lies close at hand. He lifts his eyes, and his heart leaps for joy. Then out from the gate they ride, a noble cavalcade, guards and servants of the King with golden chains and many laurels. They cry the name of the traveller with great acclaim, and the name is Ardent."

Now Sir Constant gave a cry of pain and sorrow. "Nay," he said bitterly, "there is no city, there is no knight. Dry and barren is the plain, barren are thy dreams. There is no glory for thee, for thou art but a foolish dreamer with rusted arms. Awake, and come with me."

But Sir Ardent lay unheeding; and still he heeded not when Constant took the ruined shield and held it before him, and took the rusted sword and laid it upon his knee. Still be gazed upon the vision that was not, and dreamed the dream that could never be true. And the old man said:

"Bitterness is of no avail. If he may be reached at all it will be by another road." Sir Constant knelt down at his friend's side, and took his hands in his own; and he spoke gently to him of the days of long ago, when they were squires together in the hall of Sir Fortis. He spoke of the goodness of that old knight, of his mercy and his courage: and then he spoke of the dreams they had dreamed together, of the comradeship which had joined them, and of the help that each had given the other in the practice of arms. And Sir Ardent seemed to turn for a moment from his false dreams, for he looked into his friend's face with softened eyes, and clasped his hand with nerveless fingers; but he was not awakened.

Then Sir Constant spoke of other and greater things—of the Chapel of Voices, and the armour lying in the evening shadows, and the casement looking eastwards, and the stout heart that had won through to the morning. When he spoke of these things the eyes of Ardent came back from the vision of the plain, and found his friend's eyes, and there remained, a little dreaming still, but with trouble growing in their depths like a shadow on the sea. So Sir Constant spoke on, still keeping his hand upon him, and told of the Star that came to the head of the casement. He told of the glory of the Star, how it grew in the darkness until it seemed to be a jewel in a thorny crown above a Face Divine. He began to tell of the Face, how it looked upon the knight kneeling in his vigil, and of the wonderful love with which it looked, a love that no man may measure. He said all that a man may say of that love, for no man's words may say all: and at the end he pleaded that his friend should remember, and go once more to seek the Vision of the Face, so that the love in those eyes divine should not be mocked and fruitless.

"For though my love for thee is great," he said, "it is but a shadow of that love. And He who loves thus is waiting, waiting, for the strong knight who went forth for Him. Surely He shall not wait in vain?"

Now long before Constant had come to an end the face of Sir Ardent was changed. Its foolish smile was gone, and the last of the dream had vanished from his troubled eyes. With an awakened mind he followed the story, and trod once more the path of the lonely chapel, knelt once more by the silent armour, looked once more for the Star in the casement. Thereafter he sat with quivering lips in silence, but listening intently; so the Face grew before him, and the love in the eyes, the love which may not be measured And once more the glory of the Vision swept over him, and drove his false dreams away forever, Then be gave a great cry "Oh, my Lord! my Lord!"

III

Then Sir Constant rose, and lifted him up, and embraced him: but Sir Ardent, once awakened, was as a man mad. He saw his friend's arms, strong and clean and knightly, and he looked upon his own rusted mail with terror and dismay. He seized the sword, and drew it, and flung it from him, and he wept over the shield so sadly dishonoured. He looked out beyond the wall and saw a barren plain without a shadow of a dream, and he looked about him at the garden and the house and the flowers of idle fancy. And he groaned and said, "I am undone!"

"Nay," cried Sir Constant. "It is not yet too late, or I could not be here. Take up thy arms, and we will leave this deadly city together."

But Sir Ardent turned to the old man. "Guide and counsellor scorned," he said, "what hast thou to say to me? Am I not lost forever?

"Thou hast done ill," said the old man sternly. "Is there not a grievous story in thy rusted arms and wasted days? But the King is merciful, and it is not too late until He has spoken the word. I am His messenger and the messenger of mercy. But thy course is clear, to don thy arms and leave the city, and once more attempt the Splendid Way. Then shalt thou be in the path of the King's good pleasure."

Then Sir Ardent wept, for his content was gone and his self esteem a broken thing; but in his weeping he went to his armour, and took up the pieces, and began to put them on with unready fingers and with stumbling haste. Sir Constant aided him, and the old man helped him also, so that presently the pieces were in place; but it was a sore thing to see how hard it was for him to bear them, and how cumbrous they seemed, such was the deadly work upon him of those long months in the City of Good Intent. He wept again as he strove to burnish them, so that his tears fell upon the shield of shame; but his friends heartened him as they might, so that at last he was mailed and helmed. Then they led him out through the garden and the house, through the long sunny ways of the city to the fair gate of false promises.

Now the city was as before, fair and green and peaceful, but it had no longer any power of enchantment. Never more would its spells have sway over the knight who had been awakened, and Sir Constant was so moved by his friend's despair that he only desired to leave the place forever. So with haste they pressed through the sunny ways, speaking to no man as they passed: but there were dreamers who saw them go, the knight in shining arms and the knight in rusted mail, and stood and watched with strangely troubled gaze. And thereafter, it is said, others were awakened, and presently armed themselves also and pursued their journey. For the good knight who does a stout deed makes the whole world his debtor.

So they came to the gate, and passed out to the stony paths and the fresh breezes of the Splendid Way; and there by the lodge of the Bell they said farewell to the old man its guardian, Ere they went he blessed Sir Constant for his deed, and then Sir Ardent knelt before him, and he blessed him also, "Thou shalt be a faithful knight hereafter," he said. "And by the King's grace thou shalt be glorious yet. For the Way is a long way, and thou art needed for many battles. Nor is it day's end until the sunset hour."

So he speeded them both, and stood and watched them as they passed from the city into the way that marched beyond. And presently when he was lost to sight, they surely heard him, for the great bell pealed and sang, clanging its message to the city of dreams. Once more, from a little hill, they saw that city again, lying still and white in the evening sunshine, as fair a place as any man may see: but in the King's counsel it is written down a City Dangerous, for Duty waits without and calls in vain.

Then Ardent, heavy hearted, turned away, sore for the rusted armour and the wasted days: but as he turned Sir Constant saw his shield, and lo! the lost Emblem of the King was shining once more through its veil of dishonour. For the heart's tears of sorrow had fallen upon the shield, and where they had fallen they had burned away the shame and stain.

IV. THE ADVENTURE OF THE WOOD OF BEASTS

I

THE Hall of the Glowing Heart stood in the depths of the Valley of Toil, a place of comfort and desire in a too cheerless land. In the well-tended garden grew the tree with the leaves of healing, the many precious herbs of ease, and all those blooms whose beauty and perfume cheer the soul of man. In the midst stood the Hall, with the Emblem of the Great King above the door for all to see. To many a tired eye and wounded spirit this was the fairest sight that the Valley could show.

The lord of the hall was the noble Amicus, who found his joy in serving the King by serving His people. The Emblem was the master-key to all he had, from the plenty of his table to the richer treasures of his heart. Nor was he poor in any good thing, for his deeds had long been known to the Great King through those who had found harbourage and healing within his doors. Therefore had the lord of the Hall been daily enriched by the royal favour, in wealth of soul and estate and in the precious balm of happiness. Giving freely of all that he had, he had learned that the Great King will be no man's debtor.

Sir constant came to this place soon after his battle with the Black Knight, while his heart was still uplifted by his victory. He was welcomed with honour, and at first felt nothing but joy in the right noble company which had sought that day the hospitality of Amicus. Yet ere the evening was past his joy was over-clouded, and peril lay about his path once more.

Among the guests that day were two famous knights of the Splendid Way. One of these was the aged and gallant Sir Valoris, whose face was lined with the wear of years and whose hair was snowy-white, but whose eye had the light of eternal youth. If his strength had sunk with time, this loss was well repaid by skill in the use of arms, and there was no knight more to be feared in battle, more to be trusted in the thorny way of leadership. Sir Constant looked upon him with reverence, but not without self-abasement; for when he heard that good knight's story, small indeed seemed his own endeavours. Moreover, Sir Valoris was a cousin of his own lord, Sir Fortis, a second claim to love and worship.

But there was also at the house of Amicus another knight of renown, Sir Felix of the Clean Heart. He was a knight of such purity and power that perils which had broken other men held little dread for him. It was said that his shield had never been dimmed, and there was a glory in his face as of one who saw his King always and knew His most sacred counsels. He had been given at last the governance of a great city, and was now on his way to his post, resting at the Hall of the Glowing Heart with the friend whose comradeship he had ever loved. By the will of all he sat at the right hand of Amicus, honoured for his own sake and his King's. Of all who sat and honoured him, none was more generous at the first than Constant, who loved Sir Felix for the glory of his face and for the greater glory he had won in the Royal Service. But while he sat and watched him there came to his ear a whisper, gentle and low, but deadly clear. "Some good knights come by great honours with wondrous ease," said the whisperer: and when the knight turned to see, he found that the speaker was a knight's squire, fair and quiet of mien, clad in a green tunic and armed with a dagger. In that moment he spoke and was gone, lost among the servitors at the door: but he left his whisper in our good knight's ear, and thereafter the feast was tainted with bitterness.

This bitterness remained throughout the night, and did not depart with the coming of day. He had therefore no heart to meet Amicus and his guests, and resolved to leave before he should see them: so when he had armed himself he sought the steward, and by him sent words of farewell and gratitude to his host and the knights of the fellowship. When this was done he took once more the road through the Valley.

But an hour later the steward sought his master to tell him of this and another matter: whereupon Amicus hastened to find Sir Valoris and Sir Felix, who were preparing to depart. "I am troubled greatly," he said. "Sir Constant set out an hour ago, and I fear that he may encounter sore peril by the way."

"How may this be?" cried Sir Valoris. "Is there any aid that we may give? For I loved the young knight much, and would have companied with him."

"What I dread," said Amicus, "is the cunning of the evil brood of the Black Knight. They have holds in this region, and it is said that one of them was in this house but yesterday, standing near Sir Constant while he sat at table. He had a disguise of harmlessness, but my servants declare that they marked him well. I fear that Sir Constant may be waylaid."

The two knights called for their arms. "We will go together," said Sir Felix. "The duty were plain even if there were no joy in it. But I also loved Sir Constant, and could not wish a better comrade."

Then Amicus went to a cabinet of precious things, and took therefrom a small phial. "Here is an elixir," he said, "which we distil from the goodly herbs in our garden. It is most potent for comfort and healing, if that young knight be in need, give him of this in the King's Name."

"In the King's Name," said Sir Valoris reverently: and he placed the phial in his bosom.

II

Some time after he left the hall of The Glowing heart Sir Constant found a man sitting by the wayside. This man saluted him courteously, and when his greeting was returned, rose to walk with him. Then the knight knew him.

"Surely I saw thee yesterday at the house of Amicus?" he said.

"Even so," answered the squire. "Sent by my lord with a greeting, I stayed among the guests to see the renowned Sir Felix. But I left full early, having need to return."

They went on together, and in a little he began to speak more of Sir Felix. "He is young to have gained so much honour," he said. "For me, it is ago and honour that go fittingly together: and I doubt if glories earned so soon will wear well."

Now the mood of the night was still upon Sir Constant, and he said nothing in rebuke. Moreover, he was still silent when the squire in green said much more of the same temper, for this evil talk found some echo in his own heart. Thus it was that the company of the stranger did not displease him, and they continued together until they came to the end of the squire's journey. There a gate and a broad walk led to a strong castle.

"Here is my lord's hold," he said, "and I entreat thee to come in and rest. Though not himself a knight of the Splendid Way, he holds that Order in great esteem, and is never weary of entertaining its members. But see, my lord comes down to meet us."

The squire's master was a knight of stern bearing and of great power. He wore a sword as one who could use it well, and a shirt of ringed mail beneath a surcoat which bore the emblem of a red wolf, clasping a dagger. Yet despite his stern attire he was most gracious in his greeting.

"My poor house is over open to a knight of the Way," he said. "Too seldom have I the honour of giving them shelter. Yet it is but morning, and it would be no kindness to delay thy journey; therefore my servant brings a cup of wine to cheer thee on the road."

The servant came, with a silver cup upon a salver, and Sir Constant could not forbear to drink. He found the wine full pleasant to the taste, and knew not that it was called Adulation potent to mislead and confuse the mind. And while he drank the Knight of the Wolf questioned his squire.

"Didst give my greeting to the noble Amicus? And saw you there the famed Sir Felix?"

"I gave my lord's greeting," said the squire.

"And I saw Sir Felix in the supper chamber."

"And how seemed be? As noble and valiant as they say of him?"

"He is a noble young knight," said the squire, "yet to me it seemed that some men win honours with wondrous case."

"Ah," said the Knight of the Wolf, "it is even as I thought. When is favour fairly given? And who can prove that this knight ever fought so valiantly? I would find by any wayside virtue and merit as great as his, but by some hap it has no city to govern!"

He smiled as he spoke, and Sir Constant found the words as pleasant as the wine. So when the Knight of the Wolf desired his company further he could not well refuse.

"Here is a wood in my park," he said, "with a broad and shady path that presently comes back to the road again. It will afford thee quiet and ease and shade. And we will see thee on thy way in safety."

He opened the gate, and showed the path: and Sir Constant, being thus constrained, went within. Nor was the promise vain, for the wood was cool and shady indeed. The Knight of the Wolf walked closely at his side, as friendly as might be, while the squire followed them; and ever as they went the talk was of the same temper, lauding those whose merit was greater than the world was aware. "And as for battles," said the knight warmly, "tell me if this Sir Felix had ever such a fight as that of thine in the Palace of Sir Joyous!"

Sir Constant heard this deadly talk and suffered it, partly through the potency of the wine be had taken. Thus it came about that he did not see how the path, instead of coming back to the road, wound away into darker and still darker depths of the wood, till thickets grew close on either side and the trees met overhead. Moreover, it went steadily downward, leaving behind the pure air and sunlight, and the breezes that blow freely on the uplands of the Splendid Way. And ever the Knight of the Wolf, conversing pleasantly, held close to his side, and the squire came stealthily behind.

All suddenly the path came to an end and and this at a sombre glade where stood a grim and frowning castle. Its walls were dark, its mighty gates stern as prison bars. No beam of sunlight might pierce its narrow casements or play along its deserted battlements, for no sun could overcome the screen of mournful trees that overshadow it: and there was no laughter of children or converse of men to break the spell of silence and gloom. Never shall man gaze on a stronghold so charged with menace and despair.

Sir Constant started in his surprise, and stayed his steps: but his guide, still smiling, took him by the arm.

"Fear nothing, Sir Constant," he said mockingly. "Here dwell two good brothers of mine, who love the silence of the wood but never fail to welcome a guest. Right gladly will they give thee hospitality. See, they come!"

Out from the door of the hold, that grim, forbidding portal, came two knights clad in weighty mail from head to foot, their faces hidden within their helms, shields upon their arms, and drawn swords in their hands. One wore armour of stone grey, and the emblem upon his shield was a strange emblem as of dungeon bars: the other was clad in raven black, and the emblem upon his shield was a crouching leopard. Nor had Sir Constant need to look twice to know his most deadly foe. "Ho, Sir Constant," cried the Black Knight; "do we meet so soon? Here is warm welcome from these good brothers of mine! Wilt thou surrender thy sword, or shall it be battle first?"

No more was needed to drive away the fumes of the wine and to rouse our knight to the doomful truth.

"Oh, fool that I was!" he said in his heart. "To heed those lying voices and so be led to ruin!"

So swiftly he closed his visor and sought his sword. Yet not too swiftly, for there was another hand upon the hilt, the hand of that cunning squire, who had crept up stealthily to pluck the weapon from its sheath. But Constant gave a cry of wrath, and with his mailed hand struck the knave so lusty a blow that he fell and lay, his dagger ringing upon the stones and his false tongue silenced forever.

Then the knight sprang back, and dressed his shield, and drew, the three foes before him; and so began that great fight in the Wood of Beasts, a battle whose scars he should bear to the last day of his journey.

III

In his wrath and bitterness Sir Constant did not wait for his foes but fell upon them mightily, so that he won his way to better ground, but soon they recovered and drew together, Wolf and Leopard and the dread emblem of the Dungeon-hold: and so closely did they press him that it seemed as though the dark wood had rendered up its very beasts to tear him down. Anon they fell back before him, but only to come again with hungry teeth and angry claws. Fiercely he struck at them, stoutly he upheld the guard of strong shield and swinging blade, longing for the Vision of the Face, but knowing well that no thing of beauty could seek him in these foul depths. Only grim and evil things were there, stealing silently out of the thickets, waiting for the moment when he should be struck to earth.

Now they pressed him back from his place of vantage, for such was the weight of the two mailed knights that they began to bear him down. At last he saw through the mists of despair that the Leopard was close upon him, while the Wolf sought an opening to strike him from behind. To keep guard before and behind was too great a task, for he was now so spent that he could not move swiftly: but as the Leopard seemed to spring, there came a sudden thought of that which was foe to this evil beast, the clean heart that knows no foul and unmanly bitterness, but rejoices in the sun and air of heaven.

"But I had enmity to it," he groaned, "and thus I am come to this pass, lost in a maze of evil things."

But at that dread moment it seemed to him that he heard a faint and distant call: and lo, far along the gloomy wood a sudden light, the flash of a shining shield. And the fainting knight gave a great cry, as it were with his last strength:

"To me! To me! In the King's Name! To me!"

"Fiercely he struck at them, stoutly he upheld the guard of strong shield and swinging blade."

The Black Knight, startled, paused in his onset, yet only for a moment. "Someone comes," he cried fiercely. "Let us make an end!" So they ran upon him together, and in a moment brought him to his knees. Again they rushed upon him, beating down furiously the swaying shield and wavering blade, aiming cruel blows against the drooping helm. But even as they laid him low a great cry rang through the glade—"In the King's Name!" and the stalwart knights of the Splendid Way burst upon them with clashing shields and flashing swords. In a breath the attackers were sent reeling back, and the prostrate knight was covered by the strong weapons of his comrades. Then it seemed that at the glory of the face of Sir Felix the evil spirits of the wood shrank back to their lair in deadly fear: and the Knight of the Clean Heart raised Sir Constant to his feet, and gave him back his fallen sword. "Hearken, comrade," he cried mightily. "This is thy battle, and the glorious end shall be thine. Strike hard and conquer! As for us, we stand by to guard against a coward blow."

At that call Sir Constant recovered himself, for it was as wine to the heart. He saw on one side the aged and gallant Sir Valoris, who was cousin to Sir Fortis, and whose story spoke clearly of the great hopes of those who looked to find him worthy of their gallant fellowship. On the other side stood Sir Felix, with the clean name and the clean heart of his own longing, such a knight as he would have loved to be but could never be for the foes that ambushed him so easily and the feet that so quickly turned aside from the Splendid Way. Yet even in his shame these stood by him, his cause their own; so his heart bounded, and his arm was nerved, and the light came back to his eyes. In a moment he forgot his wounds and renewed the battle fiercely.

But the false knights of the Wood were dumbfounded and aghast, for they had no mind to fight when there was no hope of a coward stroke. So in a little space the Knight of the Wolf was down, his strong sword broken and himself bleeding to death; and the Grey Knight and the Black Knight were striving to escape together by the gate that led into the courtyard of their hold. But there he fell upon them, and with one mighty stroke clove the Grey Knight through the helm, and brought him clanging to death at the very threshold of the gate. One great stroke he gave also to the Black Knight, so that the sword fell from his broken arm and he groaned with pain and baffled rage: but ere another blow might be given, he passed within the gate and shut it fast. Then its bars were between, and the servants of the house, seeing his sore need, ran out, and bore him in, and shut fast the frowning door of the castle.

"Once again has this Sorcerer Knight escaped thee," said Sir Valoris, "but this time so sorely wounded that he will not lightly seek another battle. Moreover, these powerful brothers of his are dead, and can join him in no further snares. But this Wood is an evil place, a place of dire enchantment, hiding all manner of deadly things. Let us back to the road."

"Aye," said Sir Felix. "These are dread foes of whom I have heard, though I have been spared the battle with them. The Knight of the Red Wolf must be that guileful champion Sir Malice, and the Grey Knight is his more puissant brother, the Lord of the House of Hate. Ill goes it with any knight whom they lure to this place, for there is no dungeon so dark and hopeless as his. That false squire is surely Master Envy, commonly called The Whisperer; and they are all of the brood of the Black Knight, whose crouching leopard is the true emblem of those evil powers that are under his rule, it is well, indeed, that we go back to the road." But when Sir Constant heard this, and knew the nature of the foes to whom he had lent his faith, what with his shame and the pain of his wounds he sank swooning to the ground. Tenderly they knelt beside him, and unlaced his helm, and unbraced his dinted shield, and removed his gauntlets, that they might chafe his bruised and bleeding hands. Nevertheless he could not face them, and the tears of sorrow were upon his cheek. "Alas that I should have come to this!" he sighed, "and that any friend should find me in such foulness. I am not worthy to bear the King's Arms or to walk in the Splendid Way!"

But Sir Valoris spoke strongly, while the light of love and pity filled his eyes. "Where should we fear to follow, my brother?" he said. "Know you not what the Lord of the Vision of the Face did, how he went down into the very pit of slime and shame, so that the foul things of this Wood came upon Him, and had their will of Him, and locked Him in a sinner's tomb? Nay, I tell thee that it was by His will that we sought thee here, and it is in my heart that He, even He came hither with us. For our way through the perilous wood was strangely lighted, as though one passed before us to be our guide." Then Sir Constant looked up, and saw a wondrous thing: for the aged knight had removed his helm, so that his white locks made a halo about his head. The compassion in his eyes was a light as of stars, and behind was the gloom of the unsunned wood: so for a moment it seemed that it was not the face of Sir Valoris, but that other Face, the Face of the Vision. Nevertheless it was Sir Valoris that be saw, worn with age and stained with the dust of the road.

Then said Sir Felix of the Clean Heart, his voice full of wonder:

"What is this shame that he speaks of? Is there shame in a battle fought so well in face of mighty odds? I tell thee, Sir Constant, comrade beloved, that though I have great honour from the King, never have I had the sore trial of such a battle as thine."

"Nay," said Sir Valoris, out of the wisdom of his years. "His battle is not thy battle, and thy place is not his place. For him the snares and conflicts of the wayside, the whisperer and the plotter and the ever-present terror of the Black Beast: for thee the Clean Heart and its glory, but also the awful cares of the governance of a city, with many eyes upon thee daily. Nor shall each wonder at the other, or desire the other's place, but do his own part faithfully and well, waiting the King's good time. Only each shall aid the other as the need arises. And I trow that at the end of the Way all shall stand before the King together, with the same light upon all and the same joy from His smile. Then is shall not be asked whether he had a City to govern or fought with beasts in a wood, but whether he was a faithful knight who ever sought to keep undimmed the Vision of the Face."

Then he took from his breast the phial of the noble Amicus, and bade Sir Constant drink: and when he drank his pain was assuaged and his heart comforted, for the phial held the Oil of Comfort and the Cordial of Good Courage. When he was thus restored they aided him through the wood again, leaving behind that frowning hold and those stricken foes.

There were noisome creatures in the wood, foul spirits who obeyed the rule of the Black Knight: but though their presence was perceived, none dared those shining shields and ready blades. At last they came to the road, when Sir Felix hastened to the Hall of the Glowing Heart and brought the servants of Amicus to aid. So in a while they had the wounded knight again in that good friend's care, where he lay until his wounds were healed; for in the gardens of that place are the trees with the leaves of healing, and those precious herbs from which they distil the Oil of Comfort and the Cordial of Good Courage.

V. THE ADVENTURE OF THE SILENT HORSEMAN

I

"I MAY not go farther to-night, for I am very weary. It may be that we shall find a lodging in this cottage."

Now Sir Constant had seen that his comrade's strength was failing, and for the latter part of the day had watched and aided him with anxious care. Glad was he, therefore, to see the white-walled cottage by the way, and still more did he rejoice when he saw the Emblem of the King's Service upon the door. "Great is our good fortune, and none too soon," sighed the aged Sir Valoris. "Never have I felt so grievously the burden of my arms and the fatigue of the road. Do thou knock, dear friend, and let us see what befalls."

So Sir Constant knocked, and immediately the door was opened by the master of the cottage. Humble was his dress and stained with toil, but in his face and bearing were mingled the gentleness of kindness and the strength with hope and faith to lighten all. When he saw the knights there was joy in his eyes, and with joy he answered them. His cottage, he said, one of the rest-houses appointed for the King's servants, and it was called the House of the Parting of the Ways; and he was a kinsman of that Master Joyous who had given shelter to Sir Constant after his peril of the Black Knight. So right heartily he took them in, and relieved them of their armour, and presently set food before them, giving the tenderest care and honour to the aged Sir Valoris. For he saw that the gallant old knight was weary indeed, both with the toil of the road and the burden of his years.

When they had supped he showed them his garden, at which they marvelled greatly. The cottage was set in a low and stony part of the Valley of Toil, near where the Splendid Way led on into the Pass of Tears. The entrance to the Pass was solemn and gloomy, but still less of cheer had another path which led away among the

55

mountains and was shortly lost in mist and cloud. Yet even in this place had the cottager made a garden of delight by claiming from the barren rocks many a tiny plot which another man had thought unworthy of his pains. These he had filled with soil from other places, and had then sown seeds of flowers and fruit. So at the last there were many tiny gardens in one, a wealth of sweetness and beauty which none could have hoped to find in such a place: and when the wind blew, it bore the perfume of the garden of Master Patient far into the Pass of Tears and far along that narrow way which was lost in mist and shadow.

"When I think of the King's City there comes ever the vision of flowers," said Sir Valoris. "Here to-day I might believe that I taste the solace of such a garden as His, so gracious is the peace that flows into the heart; from these blooms of thine." And the cottager smiled:

"When I choose and plant these," he said gravely, "I think of the King's City, and pray that I may find such flowers as grow in His gardens. Surely none could comfort so well the weary travellers who come to the Parting of the Ways. Such comfort and ease are what I wish for them, and what I seek to offer. So it may be that there is truth in thy thought."

"Knowest thou the end of that path among the mountains?" asked Sir Constant. "It is lost in mist and cloud."

"I cannot surely know," said Master Patient. "Of the many who have taken that path, none have returned to tell me. It is called the Valley of the Shadow; but I doubt not that it leads to the Great City.

"Then the City is beyond those hills?" asked Sir Constant eagerly.

"Assuredly," said Master Patient. "This I know, for the two paths lead that way—the one that is lost among the mists, and the other plainer path where the Valley of Toil becomes the Pass of Tears. But none may take the path through the mists save at the summons of the King."

Then the cottager went into his house, to make ready the chamber for them; but the two knights lingered awhile in the garden, breathing the quiet airs of that place of rest, and the perfumes of its flowers. The sun had set far away over the Western Lands whence they had come, but still his last beams were beacons upon the mountain-tops, and touched with glory the mists which hid the path of mystery. And Sir Valoris said, while the glory of the sunset seemed to linger on his brows:

"Surely his saying is true. While we keep in the King's service, seeking only His will, all ways shall lead to Him. As for me, my brother, never have I felt the King's power and love as I do in this hour."

"It is the peace of the garden and the perfume of the flowers," said Sir Constant in his heart: for with the Pass of Tears before him the Great City seemed yet far away. But Sir Valoris then turned his thoughts to the past journey, and, in the manner of old men, brought fair and pleasant things out of the treasury of the yesterdays. For it was now many days since they had met at the Hall of the Glowing Heart, and the days between had seen many battles and much fair and gracious converse. Yet in a while he spoke of days still older, of his youth of hope and the stalwart deeds of his prime. Not boastfully he spoke, but with reverent and grateful heart and with fond memories of those who had companied with him on the journey. Gently but proudly he took their names upon his lips, their praise his joy and their valour and worth the fair jewels of his memory.

"And of late," he said, "they have been very near me, those old comrades, as though the years between grew faint and fainter. In my dreams I see them, and sometimes their voices reach me in the sighing of the wind and the whisper of the trees. Yesternight they seemed to gather round me with many joyous greetings while I slept: and even now—even now—"

Then the old knight fell silent, gazing out over the garden to the hills, but seeing what no other might see, hearing what no other might hear: but presently he roused himself, and smiled, and said that they would go to rest, for the evening grew chill: so they went into the cottage and to the chamber prepared for them. There Sir Valoris lay down, covering himself with his cloak like a warrior after battle. His armour he set beside his couch as was his custom, the brave shield over all, glorious with the Emblem of the Service. And so he fell asleep.

But Sir Constant could not rest, for his heart was heavy with care. He did not fear the Keeper of the House, but rather some shadow of loss and pain that had its haunt in that gloomy pass and that mist-laden valley. Moreover, the words of the old knight had chilled him, for it was as though other voices were calling his comrade from his side, and calling urgently. And he had loved the old man with a great love, first for his mighty aid in the Wood of Beasts, and ever after for his tender fellowship and loyalty, and the greatness of his soul.

So at last he rose, and having clothed himself, sat down to watch by the sleeper. Whatever the perils of this place, they should not find the good Sir Valoris unguarded.

II

Sir Constant sat at the foot of the sleeper's couch, where he could see faintly the form and face of his friend: but he would have no light lest it should break his slumber. By this time night had fallen upon the valley, starless and still, so that the casement of the chamber seemed to be curtained without by a pall of black. There was no sound save the breathing of the sleeper.

For a while he sat, more and more aware of the spell of the place. It brooded over the valley and the hills and the Pass, it crept like a dread mist about the cottage and enveloped it. Into the chamber also it flowed, so that he could hear his own heart-beats, and the breathing of the old knight seemed loud and full of pain. So presently he found his good sword, and laid it ready at his hand. He felt that the darkness and the silence foretold the coming of a foe.

So an hour passed, and ever the spell grew deeper. There was no sound from without, no breath of night wind to whisper of life and hope. He and his friend were alone together, enwrapt in a ghostly stillness. And as the silence deepened its terror deepened also, so that the sound of his own voice would have startled him more than the blast of battle trumpet.

Then he became aware of a new terror, born of the silence and charged with its oppressive power. It was as though the spell clothed itself with a Form, and came out of the darkness of the Valley of the Shadow, and stood before the cottage at the Parting of the Ways. As it came the night held a new and terrible presence darker than the darkness, more silent than the silence. So real was this coming that he seemed to hear what he could not hear—the faint sound of a stealthy hoof on the stones of the valley: and after that fell a deeper silence, pregnant with fear.

As a sleeper seeks to shake off the spell of an evil dream, so Sir Constant sought to free himself from that thought of dread; but as the sleeper strives in vain, so he strove in vain, for still the knowledge deepened, and the fear. Out of the darkness and the silence some one had come, clothed in mystery and dread: he stood without at the Parting of the Ways, regarding the cottage jealously as though he waited but the time to enter. But when he was fully assured of this, Sir Constant braced himself, and bade his quaking heart be strong.

"What foe shall bid me tremble?" he said. "Am I not of the Royal Service?" And with that he drew his good sword and strode swiftly to the casement.

For a time he peered vainly into the darkness, which was so deep that he could see neither hills nor stars: then he gripped his hilt firmly, and drew back a little. Slowly out of the darkness grew the vague outlines of a form, the form of a Horseman, who led another horse by the bridle. He was clad from head to heel in black mail, and a dark plume hung from his helmet. He sat without sign and without sound moving neither this way nor that. His bridle-chains hung like cords of silk, and his mail gave no ring.

With chilled heart Sir Constant gazed, till he was sure of what he saw: but the certainty brought little aid, for the Shadow was a token of dread which he could not challenge with sword and shield, a peril from beyond the frontier of man's knowledge. Yet even as this truth came to his heart, resolve came also, and he gripped his sword with a stronger grip. If he could not go out to challenge the stranger he could still hold the cottage against him to the last. But he would not call Sir Valoris until need came, so that the old knight's rest might not be broken.

Slow were the hours of that nightwatch, and full of dread, for all through the night the Silent Horseman sat waiting before the house, black and mighty. No rocks in the mountains moved less than he and the steed that bore him, no shadow of the night could be more silent. At times a pale star shone through the drifting clouds, but its light found no reflection in his mail: at times a stray breeze came down over the hills, but never did his black plume move, nor the flowing manes of his horses. The breeze sighed and died before it reached that sombre form. And Sir Constant sat with his drawn sword, tense and stern and watchful.

But as for Sir Valoris, he slept in peace, and as he slept he smiled often at pleasant things. His hands moved restlessly, sometimes outstretched as though in greeting, sometimes as though to grip his weapons at the sound of battle. Broken words came upon his lips and failed there, familiar names half uttered lingered upon his tongue. And so it was through that long, laborious night, until it began to be morning, and a fresh cool breeze from the East began to stir the darkness upon the mountain-tops.

But before the cottage the night lingered as though in siege, the spirit of darkness clothed in that strange and sombre Horseman: and scarce had Sir Constant guessed that day was near but for the shield of Sir Valoris, which stood beside his bed. This was first to claim the smile of the morning, so that for a time the Emblem of the Great King gleamed with mystic glory through the darkness of the chamber.

III

At last Sir Valoris came out of his slumber with a great and joyous cry—"My King, my King! I come, I hasten, I come!" And as those words rang clear, there was a movement in the darkness without, for the phantom horses pawed the earth with their silent hoofs, and seemed to champ their iron bite without a sound. Then the Horseman, bending slowly from his saddle, peered in at the low doorway of the cottage.

But Sir Valoris gazed eagerly about him. He saw nothing of those without, but was only aware of his friend sitting beside his couch. And he said, with the smile still upon his face:

"I heard a voice that called me, a voice low but clear: but even as I listened it seemed to be many voices blending in one, the lost voices of beloved friends and comrades in arms, raised in glad welcome. But through all these voices came the summons of the first, and it came in these words: 'Lo, I am the King's Messenger, the King's Messenger! I am the King's Messenger.'

"Now I heard this wondering, and only half hearing for the joy of those other voices. Moreover, it was hushed and subdued, as though it came through the mists of sleep. But at last I heard another voice, full of melody and royal power. 'Arise,' it said, 'why tarriest thou? My Messenger stands at the door.' And when I heard

that voice my heart leaped, and it was then that I cried in answer—
'My King, my King! I come, I come!'"

So great was the old knight's joy in his dreams that Sir Constant was grieved that he must have so sad a wakening. But then Sir Valoris saw his face, white and stern, saw also the drawn sword in his hand: and instantly the warrior spirit sprang to the alarm.

"What is this?" he cried. "Is there a foe?"

Sir Constant pointed to the casement. "A Horseman," he said, "grim and sombre, with a led horse. He makes no sign, but I fear him greatly. What but evil can come out of the darkness?"

Then Sir Valoris looked, and saw that dread shadow among the slowly fleeing shades of night. His smile fled, but his cheeks did not pale.

"Give me my arms," he said stoutly, "and don thine own. It may be that the dream was but a dream."

Yet as they swiftly donned their mail he pondered this mystery-, and it seemed as though a light broke upon his face.

"True that the form is sombre and fearful," he said. "Yet how can he come except the Great King send him? Let us face the mystery, then, with a good heart."

And as he buckled on his strong helmet he said again:

"Shrouded he is in darkness, yet it may be that this is but the darkness of our own fears, and the darkness of the mists of our journey. For surely it cannot be darkness if it come from the King."

*Sir Constant pointed to the casement. "A
horseman," he said: "grim and sombre,
with a led horse."*

So by faithful thoughts and brave words he heartened his comrade to face that Shadow at the door.

When they were mailed they left their chamber, and opened the door of the house. Still was the house, for the Keeper slept in peace: and when they opened the door the cold breath of dawn met them at the threshold. There, grim among the shadows, stood the Silent Horseman, motionless as the rocks: but when the knights appeared his horses struck their hoofs once more upon the earth, and champed their bits, as though they wearied of waiting. And the knights saw that this mailed and visored form had a sword unsheathed in his right hand.

Sir Valoris looked upon him in all his terror, but his face did not blanch. He knew that the stranger waited for him only, yet bravely he stepped forward.

"Whom seekest thou?" he said. "Is it I?"

The horseman gave no answer, but seemed to gaze fixedly upon Sir Valoris through his visor bars. But the brave old knight would not be daunted by that silence.

"If thou art truly the King's Messenger, show me thy face," he cried. "In the King's Name, show me thy face."

Again the Horseman answered not a word, but seemed to beckon that he should come nearer. Sir Valoris went, and the horseman bent down and raised his visor. The knight looked up, and there shone suddenly upon his face a light, as though the sun had broken through a cloud and touched him with its splendour. Then immediately the Silent Horseman closed his visor, and Sir Valoris came back to his friend: but his eyes were still filled with that light.

"It is the Messenger," he said. "His was the voice of my dreams. Out of the darkness indeed he comes, and therefore is the darkness all about him: but I have seen his face, and I know him for the King's Messenger. Farewell for the time, dear comrade of many days, for I must go with him: but grieve not that I depart, for this day I shall see the King in His beauty."

Then he kissed his comrade's cheek, and after that he sheathed his sword and mounted the led horse beside the Messenger. Silently the horses turned their heads, and silently passed away from the door at the Parting of the Ways. Into the fleeing shadows they went, side by side, the Silent Horseman and the King's knight whose battles were done.

Sir Constant watched from the threshold of the door; and in a little while they were in the dolorous way that was overhung with mist and cloud. But now the sun was rising, and his early beams began to reach that winding way. Anon they played upon those mournful mists, so that their colour was changed, and they were glorified: anon they touched the two travellers, so that the sombre mail of the Silent Horseman suddenly glittered and glowed. Then as the travellers vanished, those beams found the shield of old Sir Valoris, the shield splendid with the Emblem of the King's love. For a moment it flashed from the mists like a signal, and then it was gone.

VI THE ADVENTURE OF THE PASS OF TEARS

I

INTO the Pass of Tears there came no Sunshine. Through all the world the red dawn glowed in the East, and the bright hosts of Morning crept over earth and sky, but they could not pierce the barrier of the tall and solemn pines on the cliffs of the Pass. There day was little more than twilight, and the darkness of night was heavy and dread. When a wind came it lost its joyousness within the border, and was nothing more than a sigh and a moan among the gloomy trees and through the darkened gorge.

When Sir Constant came to the Pass its desolation chilled him, and afterwards its spell deepened hour by hour. Cold and cheerless as the scene were the hearts and homes of the people, for there no smile of welcome no word of goodwill.

Some answered his greeting listlessly, some looked and turned their eyes aside. They had no fellowship for a passerby and little fellowship one with another. Nay, some would turn away when they saw him near, as though unwilling to meet a face unknown, and some would hasten into their dwellings and bar the door, as though every stranger must be a foe. For them there seemed to be no potency in the shining shield that showed the King's Emblem, ever a joy to men of goodwill and a menace to the evil powers that walked the world.

The day passed with deepening gloom, and night drew near with no promise of hospitable doors. It was then that he came upon an old man who sat before a cottage watching the shadows that gathered in the Pass, and so deep in his own thoughts that at first he did not hear the approaching footsteps. When at last he heard he rose hastily, and would have gone into his house: but our knight challenged him with urgency.

"What is this?" he cried. "Wouldst thou close thy door against a lonely traveller? Is not the Emblem of the Great King a surety for me?"

The old man paused, and looked at the Emblem; and as he marked the bearing of the challenger it seemed that he was shamed a little, He answered coldly yet not discourteously:

"The Emblem has no power in this Pass. Yet I will not close my door against a traveller. Enter, Sir Knight, and receive of what I have."

So he brought food and drink, and showed a place where the stranger might rest, though it was plain that few had come to be his guests before. In the doing of these things his eyes brighten a little, and he scanned the knight's face with some faint eagerness: nay, he even began to ask him of his journey, and listened while he told of the perils of the Way. Ever and anon his grey cheeks flushed as he heard of some sore fight or deadly danger, yet when the tale was told the light died away from his face.

"Sore perils hast thou passed," he said, "yet none so sore as that which meets thee now. For this Pass is a Pass Perilous in which the bravest heart may fight in vain. It is strewn with broken blades and rusted armour."

"What is the peril?" asked Sir Constant. "Fear not to tell me." And the old man told him.

"This Pass is Peril and Trial beyond any that a man may bear, and few are those that sustain it. Under its spell they see that the City beyond the Hills is a dream and a mockery, for otherwise this cruel peril could not be. No king would suffer it. So when they leave the Pass and escape its peril, they are never again found on the Splendid Way, never again do they bear the shield of the Royal Emblem."

"Then they are recreant knights," cried Sir Constant: but the old man looked at him sadly.

"Speak no ill of them till thou hast known their adventure," he said. "As for me, I have no word save the word of pity."

"That rebuke is just," said Sir Constant. "Foolish it were to despise any untried peril of The Way. Therefore tell me more."

"I speak of terror and fear," said the old man, "and the terror and fear go cloaked in mystery. The holders of this Pass are two Veiled Sisters whose true home no man knows, but who challenge every traveller who comes this way. There is no escape, for no door can keep them out: and when they lay their hands upon their prey the heart grows cold, the hand falls numbed from the useless sword, and every bright hope dies. Sad is the doom of men whom they have touched, for they sit ever after gazing with hopeless eyes into a sunless world."

Chilling and sad was this strange tale. "But who are they?" asked Sir Constant. "Whence have they their power?"

"Are they not veiled?" said the old man. "The veil is a symbol of the mystery which enshrouds them: but they have ruled in this Pass from the beginning of time, and no man may say when their rule shall cease. Oft they go together, oft they move alone, but both have might and power, whether together or apart: and the terror of their spell is beyond the power of words."

"But surely some have defied their power and broken free?" said Sir Constant: and the old man smiled bitterly.

"Some have passed on as if victorious," he said. "It has even been said that some have been better knights after this battle. Perchance the spell doth not hold all; but I know well that it is sadness and loss unspeakable."

"Yet this place is within the rule of the Great King? Is it not so?"

Then the old man answered still more bitterly:

"I have heard that the Great King truly claims governance of this territory. Look over to that hill where the pines gather so thickly. What seest thou there?"

Then Sir Constant rose, and strode to the door of the cottage, and looked over across the Pass to the hill on the farther side. There the pines stood in dark array against the evening sky, but presently he said:

"I see a wall and a tower."

And the old man answered him: "Look, Sir Knight, and wonder. Truly there is a wall and a tower, but no man has seen them near, for about them stands a trackless forest full of gloom and fear. Yet some say that this castle is a King's Castle, the dwelling of a Warden set over the Pass of Tears."

"And ye have never seen him?"

"We have never seen him. The story is but a story, the fond fancy of some too trustful heart. If the King had lordship here, could the loss and terror of the Pass go on forever? Nay, there is no King, there is no Warden, and the story is but a story!"

So hopelessly he spoke that for a time our knight could not answer him: and while he pondered, the old man went to an inner chamber. Presently he returned, bearing a sword and shield: but the sword was an old sword, rust-eaten and unworthy, and the shield was dishonoured by the damp and dust of years. None could have declared that it bore the Emblem of the Royal Service.

"Mark these," said the old man sadly. "They are the shield and sword of one Sir Pelerin, a young knight so confident and light of heart in the old days that men called him Sir Pelerin the Glad. Long ago he came to this Pass, brave in the courage of youth and sure that no power could sever him from the King's Service. But he met the Veiled Sisters, and when they touched him his assurance passed like a shadow. Aye, these are his arms, which he cast away with

69

many words of scorn. Yet no man had ever desired the King's pleasure more than lie."

Sadder than any sad tale was the sight of that sword and shield. "Truly, this is a dolorous thing to see," said Sir Constant. "But what was the end of that knight? Was he slain in the Pass?

"Better had he been slain, perchance," said the old man. "Nay, he was not slain. Let it be enough that he would serve that King no more. Think of him with compassion, as with compassion and mourning I have kept his arms."

"That will I do," said Sir Constant; and heavily he spoke, for the dread of the Pass was strong upon his spirit, and his heart was sore for Sir Pelerin the Glad. Yet at last he remembered how the Star had shone for him often in the sorest need: so he bade his spirit be strengthened and sought to speak bravely in this house of fear.

"Here are mystery and dread," he said, "and sadness beyond measure. Nevertheless even in this Pass will I maintain the honour of the King's Service and the truth of His power."

The old man sat with his head bowed, and seemed to mourn in his memories. Yet as Sir Constant spoke so bravely his heart was a little stirred, and his hand shook upon the hilt of the lost Sir Pelerin. But only for a moment, for afterwards he said with a sigh:

"Alas, thou hast not known the touch of the Veiled Sisters. But midnight comes!"

II

Night reigned without a star in the Pass of Tears, and hour by hour its spell of silence and solitude grew deeper. At an hour before midnight Sir Constant rose, and armed himself, and thereafter sat with his shield upon his arm and his sword drawn. "For I will not be taken unaware," he said, "or without the signs of my Service upon me."

"This must be well," sighed the old man, "for watchfulness is as surely a law of battle as bravery is. Alas, not thus did Sir Pelerin. So sure was his confidence that he despised the peril in which he stood."

Thereafter they sat conversing a little, but chiefly waiting and listening: and at the stroke of midnight there was a low moaning through the gorge, as though the watchful pines wailed a warning of the terror that came. The old man trembled, and looked fearfully at the barred door: then came a faint sound of footsteps, and the moaning of the pines died away in a strange, dread stillness.

Then Sir Constant stood up, with his shield dressed and his sword drawn: but the Veiled Sisters were already there. Two they were, one robed in black robes and the other in grey garments whose misty outlines seemed to mingle with the shadows in the chamber. The one of sombre hue stood at his side, and laid her hand upon his heart, regardless of the glory of the shield: and at that touch he shook in his armour, and all his world reeled and swayed. His heart was chilled, his eyes were dimmed, almost the good sword slipped from his nerveless fingers. His lips were parted but he had no words, and his cheeks were blanched with fear and despair. The city of his dreams was gone, and those Eastern Hills were fabrics of the clouds, beautiful but false; the Splendid Way was a folly forlorn, and the tales of gallant deeds but the legends that win the fancy of a child.

"Nay!" said his quivering heart, "if there were a Great King, this evil could not be!"

Nor was there an answer to the gibe, and he knew that like those others he must now sit forever looking with darkened eyes into a sunless world.

Seeing his face, the grey old man moaned again and bowed his head: and the one who had touched him spoke to the other sister.

"Sister, I have touched this heart and it is ours."

"It is ours," said the Grey Sister, "and I leave it nevermore."

Then the Veiled Sisters turned, as though to leave the chamber: but now our knight fought back along a steep path of anguish to memory and courage. He was as one who battles with surging waves to keep his head above them, so that he may glimpse the shore. Well it was for him in that hour that he had donned his arms, for they did much to hearten him. Their touch told of battles almost as deadly as this, yet in the end victorious; so that hope stirred once more, and courage held back that cold tide of despair. Then he lifted his eyes, and lo, the casement of the cottage, black as the blackest night, but in the blackness a gleam, as of a star faint and distant. It could not be a star, for over against the casement stood the mighty Hill of Pines, trackless and dread: but a star it was to him, of joy and strength and aid, like the shield of Sir Felix in the Wood of Beasts. So his challenge rang out, sudden, clear, and strong:

"Stand and answer me! Why are ye come? By whom are ye sent to trouble us? I am a knight of the Great King. In the King's Name, speak!"

Then the old man looked up, amazed: in his amazement he seemed to echo our knight's cry, for he said strangely: "Aye, I am a knight of the Great King. In the King's Name, speak! But the challenge rang out with mystic power, and the robes of the Dark Sisters quivered among the shadows. Then out of the shadows they answered, in one sad voice:

"In that Name we answer, for the Great King hath power even in this Pass. Darest thou follow us whither we go?"

Then Sir Constant rejoiced, for it seemed in that moment that the power of the Great king filled the chamber. Almost eagerly he stepped forward to follow: but then the old man of the cottage stayed him by an urgent and pitiful cry:

"Oh, my good comrade, leave me not alone. For I am he that was once Sir Pelerin the Glad!"

Then was Sir Constant filled with compassion, a flood so warm that it drove the last dread from his heart. "Nay," he said, "I will not leave thee, for thou shalt go with me. But bring out thy mail, for none may dare the Pass unarmed."

So Sir Pelerin brought his armour, so long unused, and Sir Constant helped him to buckle it in place. Little skill had the old man, and much shame, and ever and anon the tears filled his eyes and hindered him: but in a while his bowed form was cased in gallant steel again, his grey head helmed, and on his arm he bore the weighty shield of the King's Service. With pain he bore it, yet heartened mightily by his comrade's love; and when he was fully mailed Sir Constant spoke to the Veiled Sisters waiting in the shadows:

"Lead on," he said. "In the King's Name we follow."

III

Now it was well past midnight of a cold and cheerless night, and the aspect of the Pass was dark and daunting. There was a faint wailing and whispering of the pines above them, a lone and chilling murmur of a stream below: but hope had shone bravely out of the darkness of fear, and though the path was sorely broken and troublous, they followed stoutly.

From the door their way led downwards to the depths of the Pass, where the stream moaned and murmured. As they drew near, its moaning deepened: then the old man trembled, for that voice had haunted him through night and day for many years. But the Veiled Sisters went on till they were at the verge of the unseen water; and still they went on, and lo, the still and deadly waters were about their feet, for they were crossing the stream by stepping-stones that made a ford even in the depths of the Pass. And the old man said:

"These many years have I been a dweller, yet I knew not of this ford."

So they crossed the stream unharmed, and began to ascend the hill on the other side. Steep it was and dolorous, and the gloom of the forest was unbroken. Soon the great trees whispered faintly all about them, and gathered like ghostly sentinels beside the path: but surely and steadily the Veiled Sisters went on, and something of peace came when the moan of the dark stream ceased.

"It seemed a trackless forest," said the old man, "so all these years I have never dared it. Yet there is a way."

"Aye," said Sir Constant. "But there is more. Once I saw a light among the trees, as of a distant star. Surely it is the light I saw from thy window when the great fear had almost overwhelmed me."

Then the old man strove to raise his head; and often after that he sought to pierce the gloom before them, despite the toil of the way and the weight of his mail. And at last he said: "I saw a light even then. It must be from the tower of the Warden's castle. Never have I seen this before. In the Pass we never look up, and when night comes we bar our doors in fear and dread."

Still the Veiled Sisters led on in silence through the forest and the night; and at last it was plain that they led to the place upon the topmost cliff where the castle stood. And ever the light shone more steadily, till it was greater than a star. Then over the crest of the hill came a gentle breeze to play upon the old man's withered temples, and when the knights felt it they thought of morning over the Eastern Hills: but it was morning also in the Pass of Tears, for then they came out of the pines to the crest of the hill. And lo, on the other side of the hill the sun was rising over a fair wide plain in all the dazzling glory of a new day.

Here was their wonder great indeed, for on the crest of the hill stood the Warden's castle, with soaring turrets and massy battlements, a place of royal power. On the tallest tower was placed a crown of gold, plaited in the semblance of thorns: and it was the gold and jewels of this crown that caught the beams of the sun, and gave the beacon-light which they had seen in the Pass. So it was that the symbol of royal pain and royal triumph was in the Pass of Tears a star of hope and comfort.

Here the two knights would have paused to gaze, filled with joy; but still the Veiled Sisters passed on, towards the castle gate. In the light of that glad morning their terror was gone and their sombre robes were white as morning mists.

Then forth from the open gates came the Warden of the Pass of Tears, walking to meet them. His bearing was of great majesty, yet passing gentle, and when Sir Pelerin saw his face his heart was overcome. He gave a great cry, and ran, and fell at the Warden's feet, with hands clasped and head bowed low; and the Warden laid his hand upon his head with great tenderness, so that the old knight shook with mingled joy and shame. Then the Warden said to the Veiled Sisters, who stood by:

"Sisters of Sorrow and Pain, show your faces that he may fear you no more."

"Thou hast conquered and we obey," said the Veiled Sisters. And they drew back their veils, so that the terror of their spell passed away forever. For the light of the Warden's face fell upon those dread features, so that the anguish of Pain was softened into peace, and the bitterness of Sorrow was changed into the sadness of fond yearning. But the darkness which had been theirs lingered for a moment upon the brows of the Warden, like the shadow of a fleeting cloud upon a quiet sea.

On the crest of the hill stood the Warden's castle.

Then the old man cried, remembering the darkened years:

"They that dwell in the Pass, oh that they might know!"

But the Warden answered, with great yearning in his voice:

"The mystery of the Pass is the mystery of death, and these are the Sisters of that mystery. Yet they also, though they have great power, are under the King's rule, and it is commanded that if any in the Pass speak to them in the King's Name they must lead him to my presence. For in the King's power I have conquered these, and they must obey. And here I dwell ever and wait, while the stars by night and the sun by day make my crown a guiding light. But men's eyes, clouded by the darkness of the Pass, will not see."

"My lord, my lord!" said the old man sorely.

"And oft," said the Warden, "when the Veiled Sisters have passed, I walk among the dwellings in the night, and knock and wait at the doors. If any open to me I go in and give them peace, afterwards leading them out of the Pass to the hills beyond. But men bar their doors, and I linger in vain until the morning break, knocking and waiting."

"Oh, my lord," said the old man, "oft have I heard a low knocking in the dead of night, but in my fear and bitterness I would not open. Yet now I see that if I had opened I would have found thee there!" And he covered his face again in shame.

"Nay," said the Warden, "all is now well, and once more shalt thou be Sir Pelerin the Glad." And then to the Veiled Sisters he said: "Go back to your own place for yet a little longer. It is the King's will."

So the two veiled their faces, and turned, passing into the forest. As they went the glory of the Warden's presence faded away from their garments, which became dark and misty as before. For still they must walk in the Pass of Tears, the two sisters, Sorrow and Pain, until the day come when the Great King shall bid them pass away forever.

But old Sir Pelerin knelt at the Warden's feet. In his joy he would have knelt there forever. And the Warden smiled upon Sir Constant, saying:

"I sought him long, for I loved him. To me thou hast been as hands and feet by thy good courage. But no man may conquer a peril of the Splendid Way without saving a brother also."

Then the day spread wider, the last mists fled before it, and its splendour touched the face of the Warden, full of majesty and compassion and with scars upon the brows. These are the Scars of ancient thorns, and they shall never pass away: for they are a sign to all mankind that the Warden himself has faced the direful peril of the Pass of Tears and knows the utmost of its power.

VII THE ADVENTURE OF THE NAMELESS KNIGHT

I

IT was not always that the Splendid Way was a difficult way and perilous. Even in the Valley of Toil there were days of fair travelling, with soft green sward beneath the feet and the music of sunny streams for joyous company. There were nights also of sweet and dreamless rest, when the stars above were kindly sentinels and the breath of the night breeze was a breath of peace.

So it was when Sir Constant came to the Place of Fair Waters. Through the valley ran a broad and pleasant stream, bordered by spacious meadows. Lovely were the waters of that stream, and noble was their bounty; and there were many flocks upon those meadows, for the stream made for them a home of peace and plenty.

On the second day he had passed this region and had entered the stern and rugged hills above the valley. The broad stream was now but a voice among the rocks, while the meadows of plenty were far behind. Then it was that he had this adventure of the Knight Nameless.

Close beside the way was a little hill, and in the shelter of the hill a kept and guarded well. There was a seat beside the well, and a hut, the dwelling of the Well-warden; but the place was lonely, shadowed by frowning hills and far away from the laughter and sunshine of the Fair Waters.

It was high noon when Constant came to this place, and he turned aside to the well with a glad heart: but when his footsteps sounded upon the stones the door of the hut was thrown wide, and a man came hastily forth to meet him. This was an aged man, meanly clad and so feeble that he stumbled as he walked: yet there was still a

79

glow in his heart, and when he saw the Shield of the Royal Service his pale cheeks flushed.

"Oh, my good lord!" he cried. "Art thou a knight of the Splendid Way?"

Then said our knight: "I am of the Great King's Service, and my name is Constant. It was my desire to rest awhile by this well."

With great gladness the old man welcomed him, saying with quavering tongue that he had never found greater joy in greeting any traveller. He bade him sit down on the seat beside the well, and then brought from the hut two water-vessels and a store of food.

"Eat, Sir Constant, and drink," he said.

"But first look into the water and see that it is pure."

The knight looked down into the deep and shadowed water. "What seest thou?" quavered the old man. "Is the water pure?"

"It is pure," answered Sir Constant, "for in its depths I see plainly the Emblem of the Great King."

"Then shalt thou drink in His Name," said the old man. "For this is one of His wells."

So they refreshed themselves together, sitting there in the shadow of the hill; and the old Well-warden began to ask Sir Constant of his journey. With eager tongue he questioned him, and again his sunken cheeks flushed when he heard of the perils of the Way, of the glory of Sir Felix and Sir Valoris. He seemed to love these tales, and they could not weary him: yet when they were told a sudden silence fell. The Warden's cheeks were pale once more, and instead of eagerness his eyes were filled with a strange, sad yearning: and as a child a little afraid, he put out his hand to touch the shield of many battles.

Anon Sir Constant spoke of the Star of the Casement and the Vision of the Face, the Warden hearing him with eager wonder: and when this was told the old man said:

"The Star is the sign for the loyal heart of knighthood, and the Vision is the guide to high endeavour. I would have loved to be a knight, but that honour was not for me: yet I, even I, have dreamed that I saw the Star and the Face. Once when I looked for the King's Emblem in the silent depths of the well it seemed to me that a strange, bright star shone there at the head of the Emblem; and once when I had seven lowly travellers at my table here, I deemed that one face shone with a great glory. Yet it must have been a dream, for when I looked again I saw but a shepherd from some distant pasture."

Now there was truth in his voice and in his faded eyes, though strange it seemed that one so lowly should dream of the Star and the Face. Then the Warden said again, wistfully:

"My time is far spent, and soon I must give my task to another. In this hour hast thou come, and I ask this one thing of thee—that thou remain with me until the end."

"Good brother and comrade," said Sir Constant, "is that all that I may do?"

"It is all," answered the Warden; and so it was agreed between them.

Thus it was that Sir Constant came break his journey at the lonely well, his heart full of compassion and wonder. That day he stayed there, and through the night: and for those hours he was warden of the Warden, caring gently for the old man who was too weak to care for himself.

In those hours there was much pleasant converse, for in his forty years the old man had given shelter to many, both lowly and gentle, strong and weak, old and young. But Constant did not speak of himself and his adventures save as the old man questioned him: for when they came to these things he saw in his eyes that shadow of wonder and wistfulness which he had seen in the first telling of his story.

But he found great gladness in those hours to see how the Warden kept his charge, for while he waited there he saw many travellers pause at that quiet well-side for rest and refreshment. When they came the Well-warden would greet them eagerly, going out to meet them. He would offer food and water, but ever with the same words:

"Look into the well and see if the water is pure. What seest thou there?" And when the traveller had seen the Emblem of the Great King shining in the still depths, he would give him to drink saying, "In the King's Name! For this is His well." And in his face at this saying there was such joy and pride as may not be described.

Sir Constant saw this, and at first wondered: but at last he perceived that beyond all the old man's lowly service lay a faith and loyalty that could not be shaken. When he saw this he loved him well, and wondered still more at his strange story. Surely such gifts had been better used in a nobler place. And after that it came to him often that the cry of the old Well-warden—"In the King's Name!" though but the frail and quavering motto a humble servitor, had kinship with the battle-cry of a noble knight in close and deadly fight.

On the morrow the Warden was in great weakness, yet as the sun rose high his heart began to be warmed, and he made Sir Constant bear him forth to the well-side. There, he said, he would still keep watch and service till the end. So when a traveller came it was the Warden that greeted him, and bade him look into the well; and when he had seen the Emblem in the water it was the aged Warden that gave him to drink.

So the day declined, and the sun sank in a bed of glory in the West: and Sir Constant, watching, saw a purple cloud rise beautiful and sombre in the form of a mighty horseman with a mighty plume.

When he saw this he thought of the Silent Horseman of the Parting of the Ways.

II

The last to come that way was a Shepherd, clad in a shepherd's cloak and bearing a shepherd's staff. He had toiled all day through the rocky pass, and must now seek a shelter for the night. Gentle he was and quiet of speech, but his bearing had the signs of authority and decision, so that when he spoke Sir Constant said in his heart:

"Surely, he is a chief shepherd."

"Shelter I will give thee gladly," said the Well-warden. "Here is water and food. But first look into the well and see what lies therein."

So the Shepherd looked, and when he raised his head they saw in his eyes a reflection of those deep, still waters. "It is pure," he answered gently. "I see plainly, O Warden, the Emblem of thy King."

"Aye, for this is one of His wells," said the Warden. "Drink in the King's Name."

"In the King's Name!" said the Shepherd, reverently: and after that he took food with them and joined in their talk.

"It was but lately," said Constant, "that I came from the lower valley, where the shepherds tend their flocks. It comes to me now that I saw thee there."

"Even so," answered the Shepherd. "I come from that fertile valley called the Place of Fair Waters, where I have many flocks."

Then said the Warden: "Where is the Place of Fair Waters that so many speak of? When I came on this path there was rocky wilderness above and swamp and marshland below."

83

"So it was upon a time," said the Shepherd, "when this well was unkept and uncleansed. But there came at last a Warden who daily guarded the well, and opened the channel for it's overflow so that this place might be fair and clean. So in a while the overflow became a brook, and anon a powerful stream. This gathered to its bosom other streams, till at last there was a valley wide and fruitful, through which a noble river ran joyously to the Great Sea. And so it is to-day."

The old man listened, wondering, for the voice of the Shepherd had the thrill of music. But he spoke still more:

"So clear and noble is the stream that travellers say: 'Surely this flows from a Royal Well, one of those eternal springs which the Great King has set for the help of the people.' There are the children, too, who play by the stream and cry: 'See, the Face of the King smiles in the water!' I have walked there and seen these things."

Wondering, the old man pondered these sayings. Slowly his eyes brightened as a fond thought came to his lips in words: Do they speak of me? Do they know who guards the well?

Tenderly the Shepherd looked into the old man's eyes, tenderly he answered him:

"Nay, they know nothing of thee. What they know is the King's Bounty, what they see is the King's smile."

Then Constant looked, fearing to see a shadow fall upon the old man's eager hope. But the old man was looking into the Shepherd's face, and the shadow never came again. Instead his hope brightened into joy as he clasped his hands together and cried:

"And that is enough! O my heart, surely it is enough! It is ten thousand times more than enough!" And from that moment some thought which had troubled him long troubled him no more.

Then as the evening shadows gathered in the gorge, and the stillness deepened, the Shepherd said:

"Truly this place is a lonely place. It is as lonely as the post held so long by that good knight whom we call Sir Nameless."

They looked to him to tell them more, and he told them, his voice full of tenderness at the first yet presently strong as with the ring of battle.

"When he was a young knight he was eager-hearted as the young should be, fired with the hope of youth and fortified by the courage of faith. He dreamed of high adventure, yet not for his own glory but for the King's. What men had dared he could dare, what men had done he could do: so he set out, desiring some great charge in which he might prove himself worthy.

"But hear the wonder of the story of Sir Nameless. In a few days he found among the hills a lonely outpost of the King's, so lonely that its guardian's heart had failed and he had gone away. But it seemed to Sir Nameless that the post must be held, and he resolved that he would hold it till another guardian came. But no guardian came to hold it, not that day nor the next, nor through many days: and since the post might not be left, it came to pass that this good knight held it alone for many years, unknown and unregarded. Other men he saw go by to do the great deeds that he might have done, but for him there was no release, no call to nobler duty. So passed the years of his strength and prime, till his force was spent, and his youthful hopes abandoned. Nay, better had he forgotten them, for their memory was a torment to an eager and stormy heart, a question that he could not answer. But never for a day was that lonely post left unguarded."

The Shepherd paused, as though in sadness, yet there was a smile upon his lips.

"Sad and strange thy tale," said Sir Constant. "Tell us more, I pray."

"Sad indeed, as men might see it, was the lot of Sir Nameless," answered the Shepherd. "But I have told it only as men might see it. Now hear how it seemed to the Great King, for that lonely outpost was His, and He had chosen Sir Nameless to be its guardian. 'Here is a lonely post,' He had said, 'set upon a rocky road and overshadowed by gloomy hills, so cold and cheerless that the guardian has wearied of his duty. Yet it is a guardian post for many leagues of the road. The need here is for a knight keen of honour and immoveable in courage: for in this lonely place he will be open to attack by the Black Knight, the sorcerer of many faces, and by the Whisperer, Master Envy, with his evil brood, and by that subtle enchanter, the Grey Questioner.' So the King had chosen Sir Nameless, knowing his name full well, and had shown him that lonely charge: and he had kept it faithfully, despite the torment of an eager and stormy heart, despite the daily assaults of the Black Knight, never so dangerous as when he comes disguised as High Desire and Noble Purpose. But since that eager and stormy heart was a lowly heart, he did not know that his name was high in honour on the King's Roll."

Again the Shepherd paused, smiling at some fair picture in his mind: and this time they did not question him, for they saw that this was to him a well-loved story. In a while he went on:

"So the years sped to the last day, when Sir Nameless must deliver up his charge: and on that day came the Black Knight once more, with the last temptation of his subtle tongue. 'It was not a great task,' he said, 'but thou hast served much people by it. Surely some honour is due to thee for this?' But Sir Nameless was loyal to the end and rebuked him instantly. 'Nay,' he said 'not to me, but to the King only.' Whereupon the Black Knight left him, to come no more.

"But Sir Nameless, not knowing that he was a victor, went to his rest, and dreamed. He dreamed that he was in the King's City, the City of Light beyond the Eastern Hills, standing to hear the roll-call of the King's knights. The Roll was called in a voice that seemed to ring out over land and sea, and to conquer time and space: and as the great names were spoken, great voices answered, with joy that might not be measured. But as Sir Nameless listened in wonder, for he loved those great names well, he heard one say at his side: 'Be ready, sir, for thy name is on the Roll'; and lo! ere he might wonder more a name was called, his own name. And he knew the King's voice, for it spoke to his heart and told him that he had never been forgotten. So in his dream he gave a glad cry, 'Here, Lord!' And when he cried thus he woke, and found that it was not a dream."

Now the voice of the Shepherd at the end of his story was filled with gentle music, SO that the heart of the Warden was touched and moved. So in a while he said wistfully that Sir Nameless had been a true and gallant knight and that he would have loved to meet him. But so lowly was his heart that he did not dream that he might take that story as his own: whereat the Shepherd smiled again, well pleased, and there was silence for a space. But presently the Warden touched Sir Constant and murmured in his ear:

"Who is this shepherd guest of ours? Surely, he is the one who was here on the night that brought me the Vision of the Face. But not then only, for I feel that I have seen him many times."

Then Sir Constant soothed the old man, supposing that his thoughts were failing: and as the shadows were closing down, he bore him into the house and laid him upon his couch. Then the Warden said to the Shepherd:

"I am honoured to have thee in my house this night in the King's Name. For thee is the guest-chamber ready, and this good knight will watch with me."

"Not so," said the Shepherd. "Let thy comrade take the guest-chamber if he will. I must watch with thee as I have watched with many. It is for this that I come."

Now they saw that the Shepherd would not be denied even had they the will to deny him; but he spoke with authority so that they could not do so. Therefore it was agreed that both should watch that night. Yet when the Warden had fallen asleep the Shepherd bade Sir Constant also rest for he would take the first watch. Therefore in the second hour Sir Constant sank into slumber gentle

87

and peaceful yet so light that he knew all that passed in the chamber. For the voice of the Shepherd was one that might reach men's hearts even in their sleep.

It was about midnight that the Warden was awakened, and it was a whisper that wakened him, the whisper of a name. He looked up in great wonder.

"Who spoke my name?" he cried.

"It was I," said the Shepherd. "For I know it well. On the King's Roll it is high in honour."

"What is this?" said the Warden. "How canst thou know?"

"Who should better know?" smiled the Shepherd. "I am Chief Shepherd of the Valley of Toil, and I water my flocks by the King's Waters. Surely the Guardians of the King's Wells are known to me. And this thy charge is one of the noblest and most bountiful of the King's Wells."

The old man gazed, with great questions upon his lips unspoken. And the Shepherd said:

"Never for an hour wast thou forgotten, for I came often to see him who kept the well. On the first day I came, and on every day with every soul in need: and when they said, 'Here is the Well-warden,' I said in heart, 'Here is our good knight, the Keeper of the King's Well, whose name is held in honour in the Great City.' For the King forgets none who are faithful, and has much love for those Nameless Knights who keep his lonely outposts, making beautiful many leagues of the Splendid Way and feeding many flocks by the fair waters of the King's bounty."

Still the old man gazed, full of wonder. Now he raised himself to speak.

"But, sir, I had no battle to fight, such as I had dreamed of, and my heart was ever full of discontent."

"Nay," said the Shepherd, smiling. "Have I not told thee? That was the battle of the Black Knight, never so perilous as in his disguise of High Desire and Noble Purpose. This day did he leave thee forever. But see, now, what gift I have for thee, to wear in the King's presence."

Wanly the old man smiled, yet his eyes shone, for then the Shepherd took a sword, a gallant sword, and laid it at his right hand. A shield also he brought, a shield whose Emblem glowed and burned, and this he laid at the Warden's left side. Then he brought a helmet, strong and knightly, and a shining breastplate, and laid these also beside him.

"See now thy arms," he said, "how the helmet gleams and the shield glows. These are the arms that a Nameless Knight has won, to wear in the King's City. But hearken, now, and find that thy name is known indeed. For the King calls the Roll."

Then deep was the silence that fell, while the Knight Nameless seemed to listen. But in a moment he stirred, and grasped his hilt, and gave a great cry that rang joyously through the silent house and out to the lonely hillside and the well.

"Here, Lord!"

VIII THE ADVENTURE OF THE GREY QUESTIONER

I

SIR CONSTANT had heard of dangers to be met in that region, but he could see no sign to bid him pause. The way was rugged and stony, the moorland bare and bleak, and there was a solitude that oppressed his spirit; but he saw no castle or place of arms. When he came to a high place the road went downwards again, skirting a lake that was grey and still and unlovely: but there was no whisper of peril.

When he reached this high place he paused to consider the way before him. He was weary not only from this day's travel but with the weight of many days, and he looked eagerly to those Eastward Hills, sometimes clear and near, sometimes distant in mist, but ever the symbol of goal and triumph. Yet now his heart sank as he looked, for those purple summits seemed more than ever distant. They were but a shadow of a cloud, with a measureless road that wound away into the mists. They were no nearer for this day's toil, they were farther away than on that golden morning when he had set out from the Chapel of Voices.

When he saw this his heart sank, and he leaned heavily upon his sword: for it had been his hope that the close of this weary day would show his goal much nearer. Then he was aware of a gate beside the path, and a shading tree, and a seat for travellers: and by the gate a man, gentle of face and manner, who came out and beckoned him to rest. "Thou art weary, Sir Knight," he said courteously. "Here is a seat, and I will bring thee bread and wine. Moreover, here is my garden, a poor garden yet a little refreshing. And I have no greater joy than to meet a Knight of the King's Service."

So gentle was his mien, so kindly were his words, that Sir Constant could only answer with equal courtesy; so he sat down by the gate,

90

and in a little while the stranger brought him refreshment and sat there with him. He bore no arms, being clad as a scholar rather than a man of battle.

"Nay," he said, "my house is not one of the appointed rest-houses for the King's Service. That is farther on, beyond the lake. But what I can I do, day in day out, for those who come this way. I give them rest and ease, and afterwards help them on their road. For I have a boat at the lake-side to bear them across and shorten their journey."

"It is a good and gentle deed," said Sir Constant. "Never have I felt more heavily the toil of the way and the years."

"And the goal seems no nearer than it did?" said the stranger, questioning.

And Sir Constant sighed: "That thought was in my heart as I came to the gate," he said.

"How should it be otherwise, Sir Knight? So many days, and still the journey and the toil, so many miles and still a cheerless horizon. What wonder that some say when they have come so far, 'There is no City beyond those hills. It was a dream of youth'?"

Now the words were gentle and kindly, and there was pity in the man's eyes; but Sir Constant was chilled to the heart to hear such an echo of his own ghostly thoughts. And the man said more, as it were out of his good fellowship:

"And sometimes there comes a dread lest their words should be true: for of those who pass on upon the quest, not one has returned to tell of the goal. Beyond that horizon reigns a great silence."

"Nay," said Sir Constant, "how should they return? They are surely in the King's Service in the King's City."

"May it be so," said the stranger "Yet how far away are those hills to-night!"

And it was so, for when Sir Constant looked again the purple hills of promise were lost in cloud and shadow. No man could have told where they stood.

"And now for the boat," said his host, "ere the night fall. But first walk in my garden, Sir Knight, for thy refreshing."

So Sir Constant passed the gate and walked in the garden: but it had little of the beauty he loved. There were blooms, indeed, of powerful fragrance, but they were strange to him, and he looked in vain for such blossoms as he had found in the house of the Parting of the Ways. And the Master of the garden said:

"These blooms are such as grow in this soil and in this air. Others I have tried to grow, but in vain. But await me here, Sir Knight, until I bring my cloak. Then we will go down together."

So Sir Constant stood in the garden among those strange blossoms, while their perfume stole upon his senses and chilled his heart. As he waited he called to mind the flowers which Master Patient tended in his little garden among the rocks, and named them one by one: but none of these seemed to grow in the garden of this courteous stranger. Yet the thought of Master Patient was good to our knight, for with it came the memory of the gallant Sir Valoris, a memory bright with glory: and as that memory came to him he saw at his feet a cluster of small white blossoms, half hidden. They were modest and tender flowers, with petals shaped like a tiny star, and white as snow; but he knew them well, for they were greatly favoured of Master Patient, in whose garden they grew in great beauty. Here they were frail and sickly, but they were the same flower. He told his joy to his host, who came at that moment with his cloak.

"It is the blossom called the Flower of Hope," said Sir Constant. "In the garden of Master Patient it grows in plenty, and my friend Sir Valoris loved it much. On that last dread night, when the Silent Horseman came, its fragrance was all about the house."

"It is not unpleasing," said the Master of the garden, "but it is very frail, and will not grow well in this soil. Many of my guests have found it, and have sought to tend it, but always it would fade away and die. Therefore it is not one of my flowers, but comes and goes as it will."

Then Sir Constant stooped, and plucked one of the blossoms, and placed it within his breastplate: and the Master of the garden said nothing, but smiled as he saw it. Then they set out together to reach the waterside.

II

Now the man of the strange garden was One of much thought and wise and prudent speech, and so courteous in his manner that his wisdom not a burden to those who heard him. "A little I know," he said gravely, "but where is he that knows much? The Way is troublous, with mists before and behind. But I love those who have assurance, and I seek to learn from them: therefore have some men called me the Grey Questioner. Most of all do I love those who bear the arms of the King's Service and seek His City, for their quest is after my own heart. Greatly would I rejoice if I could know that there was indeed a shining City beyond those clouds and shadows." And after that he said sadly: "The clouds I see, but the City never."

Sir Constant looked, and again there was nothing but cloud and mist where he had often seen the gleaming peaks of those Eastward Hills; and with troubled heart he said:

"But surely the City is for those who set out upon the Quest? None shall find save those who seek."

"Happy they who know that there is aught to find," said the Grey Questioner. "That is the thought that troubles me."

"But I am fully assured," cried Sir Constant.

"Happy indeed art thou," said the Stranger, "would that I were likewise! But I have met many whose assurance rested upon strange visions and voices and signs which might be but the likeness of their own thoughts and hopes, even as the mirage that shows water in a desert. Forgive me, brave knight, if I desire some firmer ground than that. For I am a Seeker after the truth."

Then Sir Constant was silent, for he knew not how to speak. He remembered the Vision in the Chapel of Voices, and the many times when that Vision had gleamed before him since, ever to sustain and cheer, ever with promise of the goal. Could it be that the Vision was but a vision, and the glory of the Face but a reflection of the ardent hopes of youth? Had some armed foe said these things he would have fought him to the last breath; but this man did not deny, and had no word of scorn. He did but question, and who shall give a blow for a question? So Sir Constant held counsel in his troubled heart, while the smooth Voice spoke on and the path descended steeply to the lake-side, and the whole world was grey as the speaker's cloak.

So they came to the verge of the lake, and there found a boat waiting. Here Sir Constant saw a path along the verge of the lake, the path that he would have followed had he not met the stranger: but by this time he could not make head against the will of his guide. So they entered the boat together, and the Grey Questioner loosed the sail and immediately the boat sped out upon the waters.

Grey and cold was that lake upon the lands, and near at hand the shore was barren and cheerless. Eagerly Sir Constant looked out to see the goal of their voyage: but it seemed that the mists had gathered suddenly, for there was no shore in sight. He looked back, and scarce had looked before that shore also vanished in the mists. They had nothing about them but grey mists that drifted idly before chilling winds.

He looked to his guide, and the Grey Questioner smiled. "Fear nothing," he said. "Wait but a little while." And he spoke with so great kindness that Sir Constant was ashamed of his own question. So he sat in silence until the winds of the misty sea had chilled him even in his armour. But the Grey Questioner said again, smiling strangely in the dusk: "It is not so cold. After the toil of the day this cool breeze is friendly and refreshing."

Swiftly the shadows gathered about them, for the sun had set: and then Sir Constant perceived that there was no steady breeze upon that sea. For a little while their craft would make a course, but then the breeze changed its direction and the course was changed. More than once did this take place, so that he was bewildered indeed: moreover, as be watched he saw that the misty sea was a sea of cross-currents which bore them hither and thither as though without a purpose.

At this he was so troubled that he spoke again:

"Shall we not reach the shore before the fall of night?"

And the Grey Questioner answered out of the shadows:

"That I did not promise. But surely there is a shore to every sea."

So again Sir Constant fell into silence, troubled by the strangeness of his pilot, yet overborne by his confidence and the remembrance of his friendliness: but in a little while his fears grew stronger, for he was aware of other vessels near. Through the mists they came and passed like ghosts of ships, but all drifting helplessly and all without a bourne. He could see but dimly, but it seemed to him that some were shattered and weather-worn, as though they had been drifting here for many days. Yet he had seen none of these from the high place by the house of the Grey Questioner. So he spoke again, more urgently.

"It is passing strange," he said. "Some of these have drifted here for many days, yet they never reach the end of their voyage."

But this time the Grey Stranger answered nothing, so that our knight's heart sank. He looked above, but the sky was veiled by lowering clouds; and all about him were drifting mists and eddying waters. And presently out of the mists came a small boat, drifting without sail or rudder, without pilot or voyager. It passed almost within touch, out of the darkness into darkness but ere it passed he saw one thing that filled him with dismay. In the drifting boat lay a knight's shield, tarnished sadly, yet with the Emblem of the Royal Service still to be seen through its rust and ruin. When he saw this he gave a cry: but the Grey Questioner answered sternly out of the shadows:

"Some set out upon this sea without a guide. How should we wonder that an evil fate befall them?"

Then the knight fell silent for a while in his perplexity, for how could he challenge his guide or doubt his word? But only a little time had passed when out of the darkness before them came a low, hoarse murmur that rose and fell as the winds blew. At first it seemed to be the voice of a gathering storm, but soon he saw that it was the moan of broken water on a rocky coast. Aghast he listened, and still that moan increased: and presently there came a cry out of the shadows where the breakers spoke, a wail as of many lost souls. It was as though some great ship had drifted down upon the rocks to be cast away forever.

He turned a pallid face upon his guide: but the guide said nothing, only seemed to smile in the darkness. Then Sir Constant seized his sword.

"What is this mystery?" he cried. "Where is thy promise to bear me safely across this water?"

Then the Grey Questioner spoke softly: "My promise I will keep. It is those weighty arms of thine that bear us down—that shield and suit of mail. Cast these into the sea and I will show thee a safe landing."

So craftily he spoke that at first there seemed to be reason in his words: but then our knight saw the true nature of such counsel. Swiftly he drew his sword.

"Fool that I was to trust thee," he cried. "Tell me who thou art?"

"Fool indeed," said the Grey Questioner, in the shadows "Fool indeed, to follow the Enchanter of the Sea of Mists! What now of thy vision and voices, and the City Beyond the Hills? O fool, fool!"

Then Sir Constant rose and struck at the evil shape: struck so fierce a blow that the traitor had been slain indeed: but the blow was vain, for with a mocking laugh the pilot fled. In a moment he was gone, a phantom that mingled with the mists of his enchanted sea. The boat rocked and drifted, while the moan of the surf swelled into a loud and woeful thunder; and as the stricken knight found his seat again he saw that something had fallen from his bosom, to be swept by a gust of wind into the darkness. It was the frail blossom from the Enchanter's garden.

III

The hours of darkness moved slowly, while ever the voice of the fatal shore grew louder. Sir Constant sat at the tiller of the boat, striving in vain to keep it steady, knowing well that without a favouring wind his doom was sure. A little while he held a course, but anon the sail hung idle till another wind came that bore him back again: but though the winds and currents were many, he knew that this enchanted sea had a drift that was the drift of death. Bitterly he mourned his leaving of the rocky path, eagerly he searched the darkness for the first gleam of dawn: and at last a strange sign gave him wondrous cheer.

It seemed that one of these fighting winds held his boat for a space, so that the roar of the breakers was a little subdued. When he believed this he looked up with his heart full of joy, and by so doing saw one pale star gleaming through the clouds. 'When he had watched for a little while he was presently aware of other stars shining and sparkling over the darksome sea. First one and then another, they came forth and stood in order, forming a mighty Name that extended from horizon to horizon, covering the firmament in its span. When he could read the sign he cried out in wonder, for the Name was the Name of the Great King. But he would not have seen this had he not looked up.

Then came another wonder, for the stars found a mirror in his boat. There lay his shield, and as the Great Name looked down upon him, the emblazoned shield caught the starlight, so that in the darkness the Emblem of the Great King shone with mystic beauty. When he saw this his heart leaped, for he remembered how this Emblem had shone for him through all the days and nights, through the darkness a great and glowing light, in battle a conquering sign. And as love and loyalty rose at the call of memory he cried out, "My Master! My Master!" and took the great shield, and set it in his place upon his arm: "For my folly I may be cast away," he said, "but the Sign shall be with me to the last. Then those who find me dead shall know that once I gloried in the Royal Service, though at last I shamed it sadly."

So he sat with his shield upon his arm and his sword drawn, waiting for dawn or doom; but now a greater wonder came, for it seemed to him that the friendly breeze which had cleared the skies still held, so that the frail boat continued on that course: for the voice of the breakers grew less and less, though mournful yet and deadly: and still through the last hours of night the breeze continued to blow, now faint and low, now more strong and steady: and slowly, oh, so slowly, the menace of the breakers sank, till it was no more than a hoarse murmur in the distance. For even on that enchanted Sea the Great King hath power, and the wind called the Breath of Noble Desire is one of His winds.

So the last hour of night passed, with chilling spray and fighting waves and wreathing mists, but with a straining mast at times, and a sail that seemed to be filled with purpose; and at last the dawn broke far before them, strange and grey. But as the grey light grew in the East it grew with a glorious comfort, for it touched first those purple hills so lately lost. Once more they stood clear against the sky of dawn, their summits gleaming at the touch of the first lances of the sun: and when Sir Constant saw this his heart sang with joy, for they seemed to be indeed the ramparts of a great city which lay beyond, a City of Light. Still was the mist upon the sea, still the battling waves rose about him: but far above all rose the peaks of promise.

Thereafter he made better speed and joyous; and soon through lessening mist and spray he saw the shore. Then his joy and wonder were deep indeed, for on the shore stood the Emblem of the Great King, a tall Cross set upon a little hill. It was both Sign and Beacon, a beacon whose outstretched arms seemed to call with urgent love to the drifting souls upon the Sea of Mists. So they stood, the signs that the Great King had set for men: near at hand a Cross with beckoning arms, and, far beyond, the Hills of the Journey's End.

Yet a little more and Sir Constant was aware of One who walked upon the shore in white apparel, and his heart knew that form, gentle but kingly. Then his shame fought with his love, and he scarce knew what to do: but when the boat touched the shore love overcame all, and he ran to the One in White crying: "Master! Master!"

Then the Master placed a gentle hand upon His knight's head, speaking no word of rebuke but only quiet counsels of love and courage. He had waited long, He said, for that little boat, and His joy of welcoming was very great. For He had known the guile of the Grey Questioner and the terror of the Sea of Mists.

And when our knight came to himself he knelt alone upon the hill. The great grey sea lay behind, to trouble him no more, and above him towered the Beacon of the King's love. And there I see it still, a sure and steadfast sign above the treacherous eddies and the cold and baffling wind of the Enchanter's Sea.

"A phantom that mingled with the mists of his enchanted sea."

IX THE ADVENTURE OF THE FLOWERS IMMORTAL

I

ALONG the steep and rugged mountain path there came a youth, swift and silent of foot. At his girdle hung a wallet, and on his breast he wore the Emblem of the Great King, with another emblem as of Wings Outspread. Soon he overtook Sir Constant, who was walking slowly under the burden of his arms, and saluted him with a smile. "For I, too, am of the Royal Service," he said. "I am a Seed-bearer for the King's gardens."

"Glad am I to meet thee," said Sir Constant. "When the heart is heavy there is help in fellowship."

"For that was I sent, perchance," said the youth. "Is thy heart heavy with the toil of the Way?"

"Not that only," answered the knight. "There was upon my spirit the shadow of a mystery and of pain. Saw you that city, far below us in the valley? I came that way, and for a time rested by the south gate. There it was that this shadow fell upon me."

"I know the city. It is from there that I come. But tell me of the matter that troubles thee."

"It is this," said Sir Constant. "In the gate of that city lay a beggar, lame and half blind, who received the alms of those who passed by. A little while since the Governor of the city came riding out of that gate with a company of men-at-arms: and one of these, having a heart of stone, thrust at the beggar with the butt of his lance, so that he reeled and fell, crying out in pain. The Governor heard the cry, but seeing that it was a beggar, passed on unheeding: and the only help came from an old dame who lived by the gate in great poverty. She came to the beggar, and lifted him up, and took him to her cottage to wash his wound. Then she took him to his home, and with her last piece of money bought him further ease for his pain."

"It was a full noble deed," said the Seed-bearer.

"It was a full noble deed," said Sir Constant, "yet none saw it who would reward her. It was as water cast out upon the desert sands, and she who loves her neighbours is left unblest while the hard hearts ride by in pomp and power. So as I came I grieved that so much of love should go unregarded."

"So it seems," said the Seed-bearer, "when the shadow is upon us which we call the Shadow of the Forest of Burdens. Yet I can tell thee more of that story. Scarce had that Governor left the gate when his horse stumbled and fell, and the rider was slain; so that in a moment the pride of life and power was quenched in death."

"Alas!" said the knight. "Now I grieve also for the splendour so suddenly darkened. But surely that was punishment for his hardness of heart?"

"Nay," said the Seed-bearer, "not in that way does the Great King keep account. Rather let us say that every man should walk in humility and mercy, since death may in a moment end his tale. But as for thee, since thou art weary and troubled it will be well for thee to rest awhile in the King's Gardens. If it be thy desire I can lead thee thither."

"I knew not that there were gardens in these mountains," said Sir Constant. "There is little sign of them."

And the Seed-bearer, whose name was Horis, smiled again.

"They are here, yet many never find the narrow way that leads to the place. Therefore they miss the rest and joy that the gardens give." Now these words were good to our knight, weary with the shadow and the loneliness of the road. "If I am permitted," he said, "I will visit this place."

And the Seed-bearer answered gently: "It is the King's pleasure that His servants should seek the gardens and see their beauty."

So they went together along a steep and narrow mountain byway. "Some have called it the Way of Faith, and others the Way of Patience," said Horis. "But these names are one." So after a while they came to a great door which opened before him, loosing into the wild mountains the fragrance of many flowers.

Then Sir Constant stood awhile in wonder, for the place was beautiful indeed. The gardens stretched away to East and West and North and South, so that he could no walls. Broad green pathways were shaded by stately trees laden with flowers and fruit, and over all was the breath of gentle winds and the freshness of morning. It was a garden where storm and tempest never came. There were many flowers of beauty and sweetness all around, but the favoured flower of the garden was a lily that grew like a star, sweeter than any lily in the gardens of earth and whiter than the spotless snows of the great north. So magical were these in their fragrance that as it reached our knight his weariness passed like a dream, his eyes brightened and his heart found rest. But Horis led him on till they came to a garden bed that was filled with these white lilies, row and row. There he opened the wallet at his girdle, and took therefrom one little seed. This he dropped at the verge of the garden bed, and immediately upon that spot there sprang up a lily like the others, as fair and fragrant as any.

Then cried the knight: "Do these require neither care nor tillage, water nor shelter?"

"Nothing harmful can enter the gardens of the Great King," answered Horis. "As for that seed, it was already a perfect flower, and needed only the air of the garden to be seen in all its beauty. But though the flowers cannot be harmed, they have care and tending, for they are the delight of the Gardener, who walks here daily. My fellow-servants and myself have naught to do with this, but only collect the seeds from the homes of men. We bring them here, leaving them to the Gardener and the garden."

"And these lilies?" asked Sir Constant. "Are they the most precious of all the flowers?"

"They are," said Horis. "There is a deed which links Heaven and Earth, for it shows the greatest glory of both Earth and Heaven. Of that deed this star-lily is the emblem, for it has the form of a heavenly thing with the deepest purity and the most gracious fragrance of Earth. Therefore hath the King commanded that when any such deed is done it shall appear in this place as a new star-lily, to bloom in His garden until the time of gathering. It is called the Flower Immortal, for it shall never die."

Then he rose. "Rest here awhile," he said. "See, there, an arbour where you may sit in peace: and it may be that you shall see the Gardener. But as for me my task is done, and I must depart."

II

Sir Constant took a seat in a shaded arbour, and there sat alone, looking out upon the garden. There was music in the trees from the whispering of the zephyrs, while the perfume of the Flowers Immortal was the glory of the place. Their fragrance was as the breath of peace, and the sore thoughts which had journeyed with him were his no longer. Glad was he that he had trod that narrow path to the gardens.

Now after a time he heard footsteps, slow and halting and an old woman came down the path.

She leaned heavily upon her staff, her attire was wretched and poor, and she seemed strangely lost in that place of peace and beauty. As she drew nearer she looked about her in awe and wonder, but also with doubt, as though she had lost her way: but while her hands were rough with age and toil, there was upon her face a gentleness and light that made it almost beautiful, It was when he saw this that he knew her for the old woman of the city in the valley, the helper of the beggar by the gate.

Then came the sound of other footsteps in the garden, and the old woman heard them. So she stood still, leaning upon her staff, fearing to go farther lest he who came should turn her back. Then down the path towards her came the Gardener, one of kingly presence who wore a simple robe as white as the lilies. When he met the woman he smiled, and her fear passed away: then he spoke in tones of great tenderness:

"What seekest thou, Sister?"

Though her fear had fled, her answer came in halting words and slow. "My lord, this is no place for such as I. But they told me that I must come hither to gather of that which I have sown."

"Even so," said the Gardener gently. "All must come here at last. What hast thou sown?"

But she did not understand, and the Gardener said again:

"This is the Garden of deeds which have given joy to the Great King. Come with me, and we will seek for anything of thine that is here."

Then she bowed her head in shame, and the tears came upon her face.

"Oh, my lord," she said, "There is nothing here of mine. Is it not known that I was poor and crippled and could do nothing for the King?"

"All is known," said the Gardener very gently. "Come with me."

Still weeping, she followed him along the green pathway. Anon he paused beside a bed of flowers, and again he paused, but ever she said, "They are not mine, they are not mine. Mock me not, my lord, for they are very beautiful!" And at last she said, "I pray, my lord, that you will let me go, for this is no place for me. How can I gather what I have never sown?"

But he still led her on, and still she followed until they reached the place where Horis had set the white star-lily: and here the Gardener turned to speak to her.

"Listen," he said, "for I have a story for thee. There dwelt in a certain city a woman, a cripple and poor. She was a servant of the Great King, and it grieved her much that she could do Him no sufficient service: for she had neither gold for gift nor strength for toil beyond the toil of living.

"She loved Him so well that she would have proclaimed His glory to the Seven Seas, and it would have been too little: but she was bound in a mean room in a mean street, and might never go away. Yet out of that denial she made sweetness instead of bitterness, so that her face was a blessing, her words were music, and her deeds were power that healed and saved. There was none to give her fee or reward, none to tell her that her deeds were royal, for that she was the King's Ambassador in that place. Nay, all her deeds seemed as water thrown upon the desert sands.

"But the King knew His servant, and each precious deed of hers was a seed for a certain garden which He loved well. The watchful Hours gathered them, for they also are His servants, and brought them here; and when they came here they immediately sprang up, Flowers Immortal, fairest of all the King's flowers. For such deeds as those are flowers which the King will not suffer to die. Nor was this all, for the Gardener of this garden was the King's own Son, and he watched the flowers daily with loving care, waiting till she should come at last to gather of that which she had sown. So as the years sped on she planted in the King's garden a wealth of star-lilies, filling with joy the heart of the Gardener.

"Then came her last day, when she sat by her door in the sun, hearing voices as through a veil, seeing the movement of life as in a mist. But even then she could hear a cry of pain, and it reached her heart: so once more she ran to aid, raising a bruised beggar from the ground, washing his wound, and giving him all that she had for his comforting. Then she came back to her doorway in the sun to rest, wondering why the noise and the tumult had ceased, while the narrow street had gone forever. For she stood in the King's garden where the star-lilies grow.

"But the King's Son, the Gardener, saw her afar off, for he had been waiting for her: so he came to her, and showed her the garden, and told her the story of her own sowing. Then he said, even as I say unto thee: 'Come, sister, gather the blooms which are thine—the white flowers of deeds done for love only, without thought of fee or reward.'"

So he spoke and ended his story. Then he waited until she should see its meaning and gather the flowers. But when it became plain to her she only fell before him, touching his feet and crying, "Lord, Lord!" and nothing more. So he stooped and plucked three of the star-lilies, saying:

"It is these that make thee beautiful for the King's presence. For the King will regard no beauty save that of the Flowers Immortal. Take them, for they are thine."

So she took the lilies, one by one. When she took the first blossom the marks of age fell from her, so that she was young and fair and comely, as pure love is: the second changed her worn and beggarly raiment into a robe of pure white, such as the Gardener wore: for pure love is ever a garment of white: and when she took the third lily it brought light to her faded eyes and radiance to her look, for pure love is ever the power that lights and warms the world. And immediately three new star-lilies sprang up in place of those that were plucked: for the love blossoms which grow in the gardens of the Great King are Flowers Immortal.

Then he spoke gently to the woman, raising her up: and they walked away together down the pathway till they were lost to sight: but after, in the far distance, there was a vision, as of a chariot of light, drawn by horses winged with fire and shod with gold. They fled swiftly into those distant hills where the King's City stands.

III

Our knight remained in the arbour, almost thinking that these things might be a dream, yet knowing in his heart that he saw those things that are eternally truth. So in a while he heard footsteps once more, and saw that another guest had come to the Gardens of the Great King. This was a man of bearing proud and stern, clad in rich garments and with jewels at his neck and girdle. He walked as one who had wielded powers so that in a while Sir Constant knew who he must be. "It is," he said, "the Governor of that city, who would not heed the beggar's cry." And at that thought he trembled, while a deep pity filled his heart.

The man looked this way and that, bewildered and afraid. Now he walked a little down one of the green paths, and now he paused, pressing his hand against his brow: but at last he came to understand the purpose of the garden, and moved quickly from place to place as though seeking what might not be found. In a little while he stood gazing with troubled eyes at a bed in the garden that was strangely bare of beauty. It was his own, and when he had looked a while he groaned, and would have turned away; for in that bed grew none of the Flowers Immortal, the flowers that the King loves best: but he could not leave that spot, so he covered his face with his hands.

In a little while he heard a footstep, and looked up, and lo! over against him stood the Gardener, looking not at him, but at the flowerless garden. Then he who had been a Governor looked upon the Gardener, and knew him: and when he knew him he gave a great cry, and turned, and fled, seeking some place where he might hide himself. Had he stayed there the Gardener would have looked up, and to meet the Gardener's eyes was a terror which he could not bear.

But the Gardener raised his head, and looked after him. Sadly He looked, but there was love and pity in the sadness: and in a little space he walked away down the garden, as though to follow him who had fled so vainly. And then our knight rose, and found the door by which he had entered the garden, and so reached once more the path that is called the Way of Faith and Patience.

The hills were bleak and shadowed, for night was near, but he bore with him the fragrance of the Flowers Immortal, the music of the Voice of the Gardener.

There still lie the Gardens of the Great King, where the white-robed Gardener tends His Star-lilies until the time of gathering. Happy are those who find the door, for there the shadow of the Forest of Burdens is lifted from their hearts. But the way is not an easy way.

X THE ADVENTURE OF THE FOREST OF BURDENS

I

THROUGH the days and the years the Forest of Burdens was like a shadow upon the course of the Splendid Way. Sir Constant had seen it from the casement of the Chapel of Voices, and every day thereafter had revealed it anew, a mystery and a menace. In the windings of the Valley of Toil it was a cloud that stretched to the utmost range of sight, and in the Pass of Tears it mingled its gloomy branches with the pines that hid the Warden's castle. When the Way climbed through sunny uplands the shadow fell back awhile, and there were days when there were some hints of beauty in the dark colours that mingled with the evening clouds and the sunset sky: but never did it vanish with the rising of the sun, never did its long line break to reveal a glory beyond. And often the Forest grew so close to the path that the Splendid Way was but a slender thread through its silent aisles.

Sir Constant knew that this was one of the mysteries of the Way, and that in the King's good time the light must shine upon it: but oft his journey was overcast by this spell of mystery and shadow and silence. So it was on that last day, when sunset found him alone upon the path with no house of rest at hand, and with the Forest close upon him. He had deemed that the end of the journey must be near, and had looked to see the Way leave these devious windings to mount the last range of hills. But still the winding way, still the stony path and narrow, still the screen of strange and darksome forest.

Now he came suddenly to a parting of ways, for a track came out of the Forest and crossed his path, to be lost again in the forest on the other side. It was not his purpose to follow this path, but he wondered who had gone that way to so much gloom and care. And while he wondered there came a ringing of hoofs and bridle-chains, and a knight with two squires came riding up behind him. The knight wore the arms of the Great Service, and when he saw Sir Constant he drew rein and saluted him graciously.

"I see the Arms of the Service," he said, "and its Emblem is very dear to me. I beg thy name, Sir Knight."

Sir Constant told him, liking his manner well: and the knight, whose name was Sir Plaudio, turned with great joy to his squires. "Mark this!" he cried. "Here we have the good hap to meet Sir Constant, the conqueror of the false Sir Joyous and the champion of the Wood of the House of Hate." And again he turned to Sir Constant:

"Well it was that we found thee," he said, "for now we may serve thee for the last stage of thy journey. Beyond this Forest lies the last green hill, and over that hill goes the Splendid Way, splendid indeed at last, to the very gate of the City Royal. And we have a horse, so that the end of thy long quest may be with ease and honour."

Then the squires came forward, and between them was a noble charger richly decked, all its trappings bearing the Royal Emblem. It was a glorious gift, and our knight's heart warmed at the sight.

"Truly do I give thee thanks," he cried. "Is it the King's will that I ride with thee?"

"Not with us," said the knight. "It is not our lot to reach the City so soon. But it is ours to serve the Knight Victorious and to speed him on his way."

Now the heart of Sir Constant was uplifted, for he was weary with journeys and battles: and age had come upon him, so that there were other lines upon his face than those of scars. Nor did he doubt that this gift was good, for he still held faithfully to the Splendid Way. But ere he could accept it there came a Sound of hard breathing and a moaning, and out into the open space came a man, stumbling heavily beneath a burden almost beyond his strength to bear. He was a peasant, and old, but above all was the pain of his burden, for the sweat ran from his face and his brows were wrung with anguish.

He came out of the Forest, and made as if to enter it on the other side. He saw the knights but scarcely heeded them, and would have passed on; but Sir Constant went to him, and laid his hand upon him kindly, and lifted the burden from his back.

"Stay, friend," he said. "Is there need of such haste? Surely there is time for rest."

The man stood, and straightened himself, and looked dully upon them. "There is haste," he said sullenly. "The tribute is due, and where shall I find rest?"

But Sir Constant made him sit down upon the grass beside his burden, and gave him wine from his own flask. And while Sir Plaudio and his squires looked on in impatient wonder, he questioned him further. And the man, a little refreshed, spoke more gently.

"All who dwell in this Forest, and they are many, must pay a tribute to their lord, the lord of the Forest: and this tribute is to bear a certain weight of silver from his silver-mines afar off and deliver it at his castle. This is the law of the Forest, which through this law is called the Forest of Burdens: and there is none that may escape it. I have been to the mines, and here is my burden: but the way is heavy and the burden more than I can bear. Yet bear it I must, for it is the law."

Then again he looked sullenly at the knights and sullenly at his burden: but Constant spoke aside to Sir Plaudio:

"My heart speaks for this man. The terror of this place is great, and he must bear it alone."

But Sir Plaudio answered gravely. "Is not of his lot appointed? Can any man change it, or should he do it if he had the power? Doubtless some sore rebellion hath brought in this law, now so irksome. I doubt if we may put a hand to it."

Sir Constant heard, but his heart grew still the heavier for the pain of the burden-bearer. And the man looked sullenly upon them as they talked.

"Moreover," said Sir Plaudio, "if this is the King's appointment, as it may be, how shall His servants even question it? It is surely not their place as loyal servants. They have other quests, and ever the King's business requireth haste. Is it not so?"

"It seemeth so," said Sir Constant. "And yet my heart misgives me for this man. How can I see him fall beneath his load?"

And Sir Plaudio said again, gravely: "consider well lest thy good heart even now lead thee from the Way. Hast thou done so meanly that this may not be left to others? The Peril of Sir Joyous, and the House of Hate, and the City Dangerous, and the Misty Sea—are not these enough for thee to show? Come, I pray, ere the day be spent, and leave this man to his own task!"'

"Aye," said the man, hearing. "It is mine, and I ask no man to share it." And he rose from the ground.

But still Sir Constant pondered, while Sir Plaudio and his squires waited upon his word. And the shadows of the Forest darkened upon the way, and one lonely star came forth in the evening sky.

Then Sir Constant laid his hand upon his brow, burdened and bewildered: but as he did so he remembered what Sir Fortis had told him long ago in the Chapel of Voices, how that he must ever seek and follow the Vision of the Face. At this thought he looked up, and lo! that lonely star, shining faintly down upon him between the leaves, from a darkening sky. To him it was like the Star of the Chapel of Voices, and once more the glory of the Vision was upon him as wondrous in power as on that night of vigil. Its splendour overwhelmed him, but more than the splendour was the love of that marvellous countenance, the compassion of those yearning eyes. As it burst upon him his heart swelled in joyous answer, and his course was taken. He turned again to Sir Plaudio.

"It must be so," he said. "I must share his burden with him."

But Sir Plaudio's face darkened. "Is that thy resolve?" he asked sternly.

"It is my resolve. I must aid him. I must aid him, even if I never reach the City Royal."

Sir Plaudio looked upon him steadily, and saw that his heart was set: so suddenly the knight reined back his horse, and turned him, and rode away. The squires turned also, and followed their master, taking the led horse with them. There was no gentle courtesy, no word of farewell, but a murmuring of wrath, and a sound of laughter and a ringing of bridle chains that soon died away in the forest distances.

But Sir Constant spoke to the man of the Forest. "Not alone shalt thou go," he said. "I will help thee to the end of thy journey."

"It is my burden," said the peasant, "and I ask no man to share it."

"Nay," said Sir Constant, "but there is constraint upon me. Let us go."

They took the burden together, and entered the forest; and at once the last of the day was gone, and they were in a world of swiftly deepening shadow. But ere they had gone many paces the man said:

"Knew you well that knight who rode away so roughly? He seemed no friend of thine."

"No," said Sir Constant. "It was then that I saw him first. But he was a good knight, friendly and courteous."

"It may be so," said the man. "I know little of things that are not my concern. But for all his fair words he was at heart no friend of thine. When thou didst watch that star I saw that he eyed thee fiercely, and laid his hand upon his sword. Yet secretly was it done, as though he feared to test thee in an open fight. When I saw this I knew who he might be."

"What is this strange saying?" cried Sir Constant. "I pray thee tell me all."

"He must be that very strong champion called the Black Knight," answered the peasant. "In his true form he wears black armour, with a leopard upon his shield. But he is seldom seen in his true form, for he is a sorcerer-knight as renowned for his subtlety in disguise as for his skill and strength in battle. It must be that be hath tried thee ere this and found thee more than his match." Then was Sir Constant sore at heart for the snare that he had barely escaped, but the sorrow was covered by his joy in the vision that had saved him. "If this is true," he said, "I am indeed sore beset. Great is my dread of this treacherous foe. Ever has he been my bane."

"Nay," said the peasant, with scorn in his voice. "Have no dread now, for he will trouble thee no more. That champion indeed lies in wait at the entrance to this forest, but never hath he followed any knight far within its tangled paths. These dark and toilsome ways, I trow, are little to his liking."

So they went on together.

II

Nowhere in all the world shall a traveller find a region more dolorous than the Forest of Burdens, save only the Pass of Tears. Even at high noon the light was faint and pale, and the shadows gathered grimly long before the sun had sunk in the west. Its ancient trees lifted tortured arms to an unseen sky, and never was a maze more perplexing than that of its tangled undergrowth and its dense and thorny thickets. Nor was there any plain path.

"Each must make his own path," said the man of the Forest. "There is no clean highway. By long use we learn a little, and so go from place to place. But all the ways bring us at last, they say, to the fortress of our stern lord, Sir Justus."

"And hast thou seen him?" asked Sir Constant.

"Why should I wish to see him?" said the man. "Is it not enough for me, his tribute and his forest? Little desire have I to see his face."

They went into the shadowed maze, bearing the burden together, but the man leading. The path was full of ruts and overhung by brambles, so that from the first the way was a broken and laboured way. Soon dead darkness gathered round them, and deep silence, save for their own stumbling footsteps, and hard breathing, and few halting words. And soon the man fell, for he was old and feeble, so that presently Constant took the burden himself, and laid it upon his own shoulders.

"It is my lot," said the man, still sullenly, "and I ask no man to bear it," but since Sir Constant said no word in answer he fell silent, and took the knight by the hand, and led him on.

As they went deeper the path grew still more troublous, now with thorns and brambles, now with ruts and mire; and ever the burden grew more weighty, so that even the great strength of our knight was little enough. In a while the sweat was in his eyes; but he strengthened his heart with the thought that if he had not come the old man must have fallen by the way; and then came the memory of the Vision of the Face, and he saw that he could do no other.

Yet in no battle had he been more sorely beset: and never were thorns like the thorns of this dread forest, for they had no pity. They tore his hands despite his gauntlets, and they pierced his feet through his stout shoes of leather. Nor was this all, for when he could not save himself because of his burden they clung to his helm and scarred his brows. So keen was the pang that he groaned in his heart, and would have groaned aloud but that he would not trouble the peasant by the knowledge of his hurt.

But the peasant knew something of his trouble, and was filled with wonder. "Oh, my good lord," he said at last, "the burden is mine, and I cannot ask any man to bear it for me. Surely thou hast done enough. Now, therefore, let it lie in the path, and return to thy Way. What man shall do so much for another and a stranger?"

But Constant said, "Lead on."

They came now to the thickest of the Forest, where the darkness was deep indeed, and the path a very pit, and the light of day as far away as if it had never been. Again the man fell, and would scarce have raised himself had it not been that Constant was with him: and twice Sir Constant sank to his knees, and would have been hard put to it to recover himself but for the presence of that man's misery, and one more thought of the Vision of the Face. So he rose, and staggered on. And as they came clear of the Pit he knew another wonder of the Forest of Burdens. Sad and dark and dread might the Forest be, but it was easier for him because he helped another. In his pity lay some source of power, in the touch of this helpless one some deep secret of comfort.

Thus it was that in a while they came out of their dire distress, and were making better way. Then the peasant said in wonder:

"There is a light! Surely I see a light upon the path! One has walked here before us, and has left a light in every footprint for those who follow him."

Now this seemed to be but a dream of the old man, but if it were a dream it cheered his heart. So from that moment he walked more strongly himself, and led Sir Constant with better spirit. Anon he said joyfully that the light remained in the path, though he could see no man: and truly it seemed to be so, for soon they found a beaten way, and saw before them a light at a castle gate, a gate ancient and moss-grown, with frowning battlements above. It was the fortress of the Forest, where the burden must be delivered. It was about this time that Constant noticed a strange, sweet odour as of flowers, and called to mind the odour of the Flowers Immortal, those fragrant blossoms which he had seen in the gardens of the Great King.

"Dost thou see flowers at our feet?" he asked; and the peasant answered again:

"The footprints before us leave a light, but this is a thing almost as marvellous. Wherever thy foot has marked the earth there springs up a lily like a star, white as snow and rich with perfume."

Then they came to the gate of the fortress, where he found a bell and rang it: and immediately the servants of the castle came, and took the burden, and led them in.

III

The lord of the Forest of Burdens sat in the great hall of the castle, with servitors at hand and his steward at the table before him. Sir Justus was an aged knight with stern and graven face and with the eye of judgment. He wore as it were a crown, but it was of iron, and its only beauty was one pale jewel clear but cold in lustre. On the table lay a sword unsheathed, so great that few men might wield it; but so mighty a man was Sir Justus that it seemed not too great for him.

Then the servitors weighed the silver, and the steward took account of it. While they did this Sir Constant marked a symbol carved upon the wall behind the seat of the lord of the castle It was the symbol of a pair of balances of which the one had been heavily weighted and the other light indeed; but in the lighter vessel of the balances lay a cross, the Emblem of the Great King, as though set in the scales to restore the balance But while he wondered at this sign the steward said to his lord:

"It is the law that the people of the forest shall pay this tribute of a burden. This man could not pay, for the task was too great for him. Is it according to the law that he go free?"

Then said the lord of the castle, sternly: "The tribute is paid, for the silver is here. How comes it here if he could not pay it?"

And the peasant cried, upon his knees: "It was my burden, and I asked no man to share it with me; but this man came, and took it from me, and delivered it at the gate. In that the tribute is paid I claim my quittance."

Then said Sir Justus: "The question is good, Master Steward, and the answer is good also: for there is one law greater than the law of the Forest, and that is the law of the Pierced Hands and Feet and the Bleeding Brows. I see that with these signs this man hath paid the tribute for his brother, and hath set him free. Therefore shalt thou make out the quittance."

Then the steward at the table wrote, and while he wrote the lord of the castle said to Sir Constant:

"In thy heart thou dost challenge the law of this Forest, for its harshness and its mystery. The law is indeed a mystery, a mystery of pain and tears and sorrow since the long-forgotten beginning, but it is not a mystery of mine. These were a hard and rebellious people, and it may be that they brought the law upon themselves: but I hold to my duty, knowing that in the King's good time the mystery shall be unveiled. Meanwhile I see this wonder daily, as surely as the sun rises in the heavens—that the New Law of the Pierced Hands and Feet and the Bleeding Brows doth conquer the Old Law of the Forest, and disarm the rage of rebellion, and win for the King the heart so hard that no other power may win it. These things shalt thou see also ere the day is done."

119

Then he sealed the quittance with his signet ring, which bore the emblem of a sword upon which a cross bad been laid: and when the peasant had taken the quittance and laid it in his bosom he took Sir Constant by the hand to lead him from that place of strange symbols, that castle of ancient strength. Nor was Constant unwilling to go, for there was little cheer in that stern hall with its bared sword and silent servitors, and its austere lord with the crown of iron. So in a little while they reached the Peasant's Cottage.

There they found his wife and his children who gave them a glad welcome and whose joy in the quittance was good indeed to see. Then the man brought water, and relieved Sir Constant of his armour, and washed his hands and feet and brows. Now at last he saw how his helper had been torn by the thorns of the forest, and his face became troubled Long he gazed at those wounds, and suddenly he broke into tears, and gently kissed the marks, and cried, "These wounds were for me!" Then he stood before the Emblem of the gallant shield, and said, "This is the Sign of the King who sent thee. By thy deed I know that He is love, despite the pain and mystery of this Forest. So let me be His man forever!" And Sir Constant and the woman and children saw it in wonder, for he was of a sullen spirit. The sight of those wounds had touched his heart as nothing else had touched it through all the days of his life.

After this they set supper before the two who had come through the forest, and it was a supper of bread and wine: and as they supped Sir Constant remembered the day long ago when he had taken bread and wine with Sir Fortis in the Chapel of Voices. It had seemed to him that one other had been present at that feast, and now it was the same. Through the dark and silent forest He came, leaving a light in every footprint: the door of the cottage opened at His touch, and He came in, and sat at the table between the knight with the marked hands and the man whose burden had been shared. With silent lips he sat, but His eyes spoke the things that could not be spoken.

When the supper was done Sir Constant went to his rest: but before he rested he pondered awhile how far he might have wandered from the Splendid Way and how he might return to it. Yet he felt that in the adventure of the Forest he could not be far from the King's Will. "Surely," he said, "Sir Fortis told me that the Vision must ever be my guide, and I saw it when I entered the Forest. Therefore in the morning I shall see the Way once more."

In a little while he lay down to sleep, fearing that the terror of the Forest might oppress him in his dreams; but it was not so, for he dreamed of Sir Valoris and Sir Fortis and Sir Felix, who smiled upon him, and crossed the gulf of years, and took him by the hand. And in his sleep he greeted them with joy.

So the night sped on to a fair awakening.

IV

It was morning, and faint and sweet from afar came the music of bells. They were bells that spoke praise and comfort and gracious memories, but ever and anon came a deeper, stronger note, as though some dread battle of long ago, crowned with victory, had been wrought into one rich tone of solemn joy.

From the place where Constant stood he saw a vision of soaring pinnacles all radiant in sunshine, the pinnacles of a great city: but everywhere the temples and homes of the city were set in gardens, so that lordly trees rose on all sides to those shining towers, and the air was filled with the perfume of many flowers in bloom. On one side there was a sea, heaving under a gentle breeze and as blue as the unclouded sky above it.

The place where he stood was itself a garden, and he deemed that it might be the garden of the gate by which he had entered the city: but when he turned to see, there was neither gate nor wall. Then in his heart he mused: "It must be that this city lay on the farther side of the Forest: but the man of the Forest said nothing of it."

There were streets in the city, and he saw people pass to and fro; and there was a sound of laughter, and a murmur that might be the murmur of toil: but it was toil without sorrow or pain, and in the walk of the people there was neither sadness nor labour, but a joy that cannot be described. This joy was the air of the city, as though it hovered and brooded over the pinnacles and gardens. As for him, all his weariness had passed, and his lightness of heart was even greater than on that day when he had left the Chapel of Voices for his long quest.

But as he wondered he became aware of voices near him, and saw that children were playing in the garden about him. As he perceived them they saw him too, and immediately left their play to come to him. They looked at him with eyes whose welcome was mingled with delight.

"See," said one, "he has a shield, and it is a dinted shield. He must have had great battles."

"Save for the children, few come here without great battles," said another. "And look at his hands."

They took his hands in theirs. "Yes," said one. "Here are the marks. See."

"Ah," said another, "but few come here without those marks." And then they took his marked hands, and kissed them; and when he wondered they said: "We love such hands as these, for they bear the marks of a friend."

When they spoke so kindly and did so lovingly he had courage to speak to them. "Tell me," he said, "what city this may be. For I am a stranger, and do not know."

Then said a maiden who held Sir Constant by the hand, "He does not know, and we may not tell him, for we did not come through that Forest. But Radiant will tell him, for he came that way."

Then came a boy, and stood before them smiling. His face was bright as a fair morning, and brighter for the deep shadows that lingered in his eyes. "These are the shadows of the Forest," said the maiden, "but they are not the shadows of pain, for there is no pain here. They are but the memories that make his joy the greater and his praise a joy. It is these shadows that make his face so bright that we call him Radiant."

"Yes," said the boy called Radiant. "But for this shadow of Remembrance how could we fitly praise the King for the glory of the Star and the wonder of the Face with its unutterable love? But knowest thou not what city this is?"

"How can I know?" asked Constant. "Last night there was a forest, dark and toilsome, but now there is no forest, but a city."

"Truly," said Radiant. "And it is the City of the Great King."

Our knight's heart leaped at the word, but then he was bemused by the sudden wonder of it, and said only, "How may this be? The City Royal lay far away over those Eastern Hills."

And as the children fondled his scarred hands and smiled in his face the boy called Radiant answered him: "Aye, far away and ever far, till the heart grow weak and the will grow weary. Such is the lot of those who shun the King's Way, which is through the Forest of Burdens. For that is the way which the Lord of the Vision took, leaving light in every footprint for those who should come after. Who should know so well the way to His Father's House? Nay, sir, this also is said, though it is a mystery which we cannot measure: that those who follow the Vision through the Forest of Burdens may bring the City near, so that its towers may shine to-day where yesterday the Forest ways were dark and dreadful. By the power of the King and His grace, it is their feet that lay down its sunny paths, and their hands that rear its pinnacles to the skies."

Then as Sir Constant stood in wonder the boy looked beyond, and smiled. "I cannot tell thee more," he said, "for I do not know. I was not long in the Forest, for it was too sore for me, and I came soon to the end. But here is one who shall tell thee all."

There was, indeed, another in the garden, walking towards them, kindly in His look and so gentle in His manner that His gentleness veiled His kingliness. As a friend He came, smiling upon the children as He drew near; and some of them ran to Him, and clasped Him eagerly, and led Him on. But as His hands touched them they rested, joy taking the place of haste, and peace the heat of a child's desire. Then one said:

"This good knight has come, and he bears your marks. But he did not know that he had reached the City."

He stood with a smile of greeting. Constant trembled, but he could not fully know Him, as though the eyes shrank from some great truth because the heart was not ready to receive it.

"It is true that I knew not," said Constant. "Yesterday I saw a great forest, and no sign of such a city."

Again He smiled. "Nay," He said. "This is the City of thy seeking, the City of the Great King."

The voice had tones like the music of many waters, and the heart of Constant surged like the sea. He feared to look up, but as he stood with bowed head he saw at his feet a bed of flowers. They were the star-lilies which he had seen in the gardens of the Great King, the Flowers Immortal. Then he saw the hands of this Man as the children fondled them, and they had scars upon them, old scars which ten thousand ages might not remove. When he saw these marks he knew not what he said, but it was some word of his own unworthiness to enter the City Royal. But He of the scarred hands answered gently:

"Thy lack shall the King's grace make good, as it is with all other men; but surely he takes the right way to the City who sets his heart against the Black Knight, and fights free from the Wood of Beasts, defeats the enchantments of the Grey Questioner and plants the Flowers Immortal in the Forest of Burdens. So hast thou come, and here I name thee comrade and brother."

Then the knight took courage, and raised his eyes; and the veil was taken away, so that he knew Who spoke to him. It was the King's Son Who was the Gardener, and it was the Chief Shepherd of the Place of Waters: it was his friend of the Way of the Carpenter, and the Warden of the Pass of Tears, and the strong helper who had met him on the shore of the Misty Sea. But more than all, the face was the Face of the Vision in the Chapel of Voices, and the eyes were filled with that love which had ever been the star of his journey. Now it enfolded him, as it had done on the night of his vigil in the Chapel: and when he felt its power the city was strange no longer, and he was at home, at rest.

"Come," said the Voice. "I take you to My Father."

Made in the USA
Lexington, KY
24 September 2017